**Cumbria Library Services**

County Council

This book is due for return on or before the last date above.
It may be renewed by personal application, post or telephone,
if not in demand.

C.L. 18F

# HIDDEN TREASURES

# HIDDEN TREASURES

Sheila Spencer-Smith

CHIVERS

British Library Cataloguing in Publication Data available

This Large Print edition published by AudioGO Ltd, Bath, 2013.
Published by arrangement with the Author

U.K.  Hardcover     ISBN   978 1 4713 4808 2
U.K.  Softcover     ISBN   978 1 4713 4809 9

Printed and bound in Great Britain by TJ International Ltd

# New Relation

Kerri Treghennel strode along the cliff path enjoying the feel of the breeze on her face and the cries of the gulls wheeling above her in the clear air. Down below, foamy ripples teased the rocks, and further out patches of navy blue darkened the turquoise water. She marvelled that she had ever managed to scramble down here and then up again without falling to her death. Kerri and Damien Treghennel, the Daring Duo, their father had called them as they were growing up.

Now, twenty-four and engaged to André, Kerri thought of her father with sadness. Dad would have liked André.

She wasn't sure she did any more.

She picked up a pebble and dropped it over the edge. André had never liked her daredevil ways, saying that a young woman should have outgrown them by now and be ready to settle down and act her age. Of course she had agreed, newly in love. But in this place where she and Damien had grown up, it was easy to slip back to their old ways and forget she had ever left Cornwall after Dad died.

Damien had found an apartment on the outskirts of St Ives, near the family antiques gallery so he could continue to run the business and at the same time paint his wild landscapes of West Penwith. But Kerri had needed to get right away to come to terms with it all. She left her temporary receptionist job at the hotel and found work for the summer at a firm of market gardeners on the outskirts of Bristol, because she liked growing things and working out of doors. Three years later she was still there. André had been good to her from the beginning and his interest in her was soothing as well as exciting.

Now Kerri picked up another stone and rubbed it between her fingers before dropping that, too, over the cliff. The feel of natural things pleased her, but it was something that Damien hated. He loved the feel of old objects. The antiques business was his ideal and she had been glad to come down to look after it for him this weekend while he went off to Newbury to spend time with Lucy.

Time to phone Damien and report on the day's business. Time, too, to text André to tell him she was in Cornwall. Pretending nothing was the matter was hard, because of what she planned to tell him when they were together again.

André wanted to expand the business now that they had the chance to purchase the field adjoining the Roseleaf Nursery Gardens. Her bombshell, when it came, might well put a stop to that, because she might have to leave the area.

Guilt weighed her down as she continued

along the cliff path to where she had left her car. Yesterday morning she knew she had made the mistake of her life in agreeing to marry André. But she couldn't tell him while he was in Switzerland on his climbing holiday. It could be dangerous.

Damien's apartment in the block of flats overlooking a small cove was a pleasant place on a late summer evening. Kerri made a coffee and carried it and the phone out on to his balcony. Damien's mobile went straight to voicemail.

'Just reporting in,' she said. 'Hope you're having fun.'

She clicked it off and it rang immediately.

'Kerri?' Daniel's voice sounded flat.

'Who else would it be?' she said. 'A female burglar clearing out your pad?'

There was silence on the other end of the phone.

'Damien?'

'I'm at Jamaica Inn,' he said at last.

'Jamaica Inn?' she said, astounded.

'On Bodmin Moor.'

'Why? Damien, what's wrong?'

'I'm on my way home.' His mobile went dead.

Kerri stared at the phone in her hand and felt a tingle of apprehension. Something must have happened with Lucy.

The three of them had been friends until Lucy's family moved up country when they

3

were fourteen. The girls had written to each other and spent time together in the holidays whenever they could, and now e-mailed each other nearly every day. Lucy had a post teaching home economics at her local comprehensive, while Kerri's gardening activities kept her busy at weekends.

She hadn't known at first that Damien was seeing a lot of Lucy, travelling back and forth to Newbury. When they told her she had been delighted.

Now she sipped her coffee slowly and then got up and leaned on the rail. The sun was slipping down the sky. The air smelled cold, and she wished Damien would come.

At that moment sounds of activity below alerted her to his arrival. She greeted him at the door of the apartment, noting with alarm his pale face.

'Damien! Is Lucy all right?'

'We're finished. She doesn't want to see me again.' Her brother staggered into the sitting room looking as if he hardly knew what he was doing. He sank down on the sofa.

'Oh, Damien, I'm so sorry.'

'I thought we were all right. I was making plans . . .'

Kerri felt a lump in her throat and for a moment couldn't speak. She was planning, too, to break the news to André that they had no future together. For an instant she felt a flare of admiration for Lucy that she had had

4

the courage to do it. Then she was ashamed. Damien was suffering.

'I don't want to talk about it,' Damien said as if the words were dragged out of him.

'I'll make a hot drink. And there's biscuits.'

Damien ate and drank quickly.

'I promised Lucy an e-mail to say I got back safely,' he said when he had finished.

She picked up his laptop.

'Shall I?'

He nodded.

'You have a message,' she said after a moment or two. 'From someone called Eustacia Treghennel.'

She gazed at Damien in astonishment.

'It's a joke,' she said. 'It must be! We don't know any Treghennels except ourselves.'

'We met on Facebook.'

'You didn't tell me.'

He shrugged.

'We've been e-mailing. She's been researching her family and thinks our branch of Treghennels might be connected with hers. She can offer proof.'

'Why would you need proof?'

'She has family items she wants to dispose of, and has no close family left of her own.'

'You'd better come and see what she says.'

Damien stood up to look at the screen.

'I want you to come up to North Yorkshire and collect. I have accommodation to offer and I shall expect to hear your plans within the

5

next day or two,' he read aloud.

'She sounds very autocratic,' Kerri said scornfully. 'Probably at least ninety.'

'That would explain why she's interested in us.'

'Us?'

'She knows I have a twin sister.'

Kerri swivelled around in her seat.

'So this woman we've never heard of wants us to drop everything and travel goodness knows where to pick up something she no longer wants? That's crazy!'

But Damien had lost interest. He sat down again.

Kerri made up her mind. What did it matter, if it got her brother away from Cornwall for a while with something to occupy his mind?

'Let's go, Damien. It's not every day someone contacts us offering a fortune!'

'A few trinkets probably. Or an item of old furniture.'

'It's worth investigating. I'm going to reply.'

She typed quickly, clicked on Send and it was done.

She remembered about the e-mail to Lucy as soon as she closed the lid, and opened it up again. She'd send a brief message now and get a longer one to her later. Meanwhile they could wait for a reply from the Treghennel woman and take things from there. Damien's assistant would be back on Monday and wouldn't mind looking after the shop on his own, since it wasn't so busy now at the end of the season, and André was away for three more days.

Perfect.

They set off before sunrise next day, Kerri's car eating up the miles in a satisfactory way. Damien had lost the deep pallor of the night before, but there was still a vulnerability about him that tore at Kerri's heart. Lucy was her best friend but at this moment she found it hard to think of her with any affection.

At nine o'clock they pulled into Gordano Services for a break and a quick coffee. Kerri was glad that she had packed sandwiches and fruit and they wouldn't have to waste any time. They had a long way to go. Before going to bed she had booked over the internet a suitable bed and breakfast place in the small town of Rawthwaite, the nearest place of any size to where Eustacia lived. Eustacia Treghennel was a stranger to them, after all.

As she drove, Kerri thought of Lucy. She'd had no reply to her e-mail saying how sad she was that things had turned out the way they had and that she and Damien were off north to visit a distant relation for a few days. Or someone who said she was a relation. That would surprise Lucy.

They stopped again at a service station near Worcester to stretch their legs and eat some of the sandwiches.

'I'll drive for a bit,' Damien said.

'You can't. My car's only insured for one driver . . . me.'

'If I'd known that, I'd have insisted we take mine.'

'Just as well you didn't, then.'

'And why is that?'

'You'd never have let me drive it.'

Damien had no answer to that and got into her car without a word. By late afternoon Kerri was exhausted, but she wasn't going to admit it and give Damien the satisfaction of saying that it served her right.

'Not so far now,' Damien said. Kerri was pleased to hear the excitement in his voice.

Rawthwaite was a small place with a main street that went steeply uphill. In this light the stone buildings looked dark, but wooden tubs of bright dahlias outside some of the shops were cheering.

They knew the accommodation they were looking for was in a side street and found it without much trouble. Kerri drove through a stone archway and pulled up in a cobbled yard. She let out a breath of relief as she saw their smiling hostess coming out to meet them. The warm welcome after the long drive was what they needed.

# At Alder Knowle

'There it is! Pull in here, Kerri, and let's take a look.'

The reservoir stretched for a mile or two on their right and they had reached it soon after leaving Rawthwaite some miles back. Damien, far more alert this lovely autumn morning, had been trying to catch a glimpse of a group of buildings on the far side of the sheet of water because he knew that was where they were heading.

He was out of the car at once and crossing the road to look at what he knew must be the property belonging to Eustacia Treghennel.

From her pocket Kerri pulled out the print-out of the area she had brought and followed him.

'It's a biggish place. There are outbuildings, too.'

A haunting cry startled Kerri as a pair of swans swooped low over the water and then landed with hardly a splash. In the reeds a little way away a couple of moorhens bustled about and a duck came swimming out towards them.

'Look at those peculiar humps down there,' she said. 'I wonder what they're for?'

But Damien's attention was fixed on the buildings on the other side of the water that looked part of the hill that rose steeply behind.

'Impressive if she owns the lot,' Damien said. 'It's a big house for one person.'

'Especially someone old.'

'With a house full of valuable objects and no close family to leave them to.' Damien's voice was sad.

'Does she know you run an antiques business?'

He shook his head.

'Not that it makes much difference,' Kerri said. 'Unless she has an unknown ulterior motive for getting us up here, of course.'

'Her belongings would have been loved and handed down from generation to generation. It's flattering she wants us to have one or two of them.'

'You, not me,' Kerri said.

'You don't know that.'

'Anyway, it might not be like that at all, Damien. She could be a fence for a gang of crooks wanting to dispose of their stuff.'

He turned and smiled. Kerri was glad his sombre mood of yesterday had lifted.

'It's odd that she contacted you through Facebook, though. It doesn't quite match up, does it? This feeble old lady doing something so hi-tech?'

A solitary cloud hid the sun. She pushed her loose hair behind her ears and shivered.

'What's wrong, Kerri?'

'Nothing.'

'Come on, I know you better than that. There's something worrying you.'

She was reluctant to tell him but knew he wouldn't rest.

'It's André.'

'André?'

'He's all right,' she said quickly. 'I'm not sure we're right for each other any more.'

There was silence. She didn't dare look at him. Only yesterday Lucy had broken up with him, and now she wanted to do the same to André!

'Have you told him?'

'Not yet. Not till he gets back.' She cleared her throat. 'It's good to be here and have other things to think about.'

Damien was silent again for a moment.

'Well, we won't know any more until we get there, will we? Let's go.'

By the time they had turned right through a group of houses, and then right again, fifteen minutes had passed. They were on a single unfenced track now, driving through fields that bordered the reservoir.

They rounded another bend, drove over a narrow bridge and arrived at the group of buildings, the largest of which was Alder Knowle, the home of Eustacia Treghennel. The name of the house was carved into a stone pillar.

They got out of the car and gazed at the house. It stood well back from the track

11

behind a low stone wall and an expanse of grass. The calm water of the reservoir glittered in the morning sunshine.

'It's an idyllic spot,' Damien murmured.

'Another world,' Kerri agreed.

They turned at the sound of footsteps.

'Are you looking for someone?' the young man approaching them asked in an attractive husky voice. 'We don't often have casual visitors here.'

Kerri liked the way a lock of his fair hair fell over his forehead. He flicked it back but it seemed to have a life of its own. He was taller than Damien and his light-blue T-shirt looked good on his slightly broader figure.

'We've come to see Eustacia Treghennel,' Damien told him. 'I think you'll find she's expecting us.'

'She didn't say. But, of course, that's her all over. Vagueness is her middle name.'

Kerri frowned. This didn't sound good.

'Ten o'clock, we were told.' Damien sounded as uncertain as she felt herself.

'Well, come on in. I'm Leo. Leo Johnstone.'

'Hi, Leo. I'm Kerri. And this is Damien.'

Damien nodded and Kerri could see her brother was trying to work out who this person was.

Leo unlatched the gate and led the way to the front door. After the sunshine, the inside was dark, and Kerri looked at the plain walls and flagstone floor with interest.

'Visitors!' Leo called, his voice echoing in the large hall. When there was no reply he turned to them and shrugged.

'She must be outside somewhere. We've been working in the holiday let. She'll be up a ladder, no doubt.'

A ladder? Kerri gulped and Damien looked taken aback.

'Would you rather leave it for the moment and come back later when I've rounded her up?' Leo offered.

'That won't do,' Damien said. 'We stayed in Rawthwaite last night so we could be here on time.'

'It was a definite appointment, you say?'

'Arranged by e-mail.'

'Oh, e-mail,' Leo echoed as if that explained everything.

Damien looked at Kerri.

'We'll forget all about it, shall we?'

She saw he didn't like feeling at a disadvantage and wanted to be out of here as quickly as possible.

'Don't go,' Leo said. 'I'll make us a coffee and bring it out here. Then I'll have a swift look round for her.'

'You work here?' Damien wanted to get at least one thing clear.

'Not officially. I help out now and again when she has a big project on.'

Eustacia Treghennel was sounding more interesting by the minute. They couldn't leave now, Kerri thought, without meeting this extraordinary-sounding woman.

Damien hesitated and she pressed her advantage.

'A few more minutes won't make much difference,' she said. 'And I'm thirsty.'

He nodded.

'Coffee would be good.'

Leo looked pleased.

'I'll not be long.'

He was gone only a short time before returning with three large mugs on a tray. They drank it seated on the low wall in the sunshine.

'This is kind of you,' Kerri said holding both hands round the mug he handed to her.

'The least I could do.'

'But it's not your fault we're having to wait.'

Leo frowned.

'I'm not so sure. She said someone was coming but I assumed it was the architect. She might have got held up.'

'Well, this is a lovely place to wait.'

She glanced at her brother and saw that he had lost his disapproving expression now. He was leaning back slightly with his eyes half-closed as he viewed the scene in front of them. The hills on the other side of the sheet of water looked inviting.

'It's a great place for birdwatching,' Leo said. 'Are you interested? We sometimes get rare ones here in winter.'

14

'So those peculiar-looking humps we saw on the other side of the reservoir were camouflaged hides?' Kerri cried. 'I wondered. They just looked like piles of dead branches covered with heather to me.'

Leo smiled.

'That's the idea. They work a treat. We've one down near the water here.'

'Who uses it?'

'The local birdwatching fraternity put it in last year, and groups of them spend hours here, off and on. We had a snow bunting last winter. That caused a bit of excitement, I can tell you.'

Damien sipped his coffee, looking about him as if sizing the place up. Leo must be wondering why they were here, but they could hardly blurt out the reason if Eustacia hadn't chosen to take him into her confidence.

He downed the rest of his coffee and stood up.

'I'll check the holiday cottage first and make sure she's not there. I won't be a minute.'

Left to themselves, Damien looked at Kerri.

'I don't know who he is, but he seems to have made a hit with you.'

Kerri shrugged.

'I'm being friendly, that's all. I like him. He's nice. And what's the hurry, anyway? It's great sitting here in the sunshine and we came a long way.'

'But not to be made fools of.' Damien

15

placed his mug on the tray. 'For someone who seemed desperate to get us here she is very casual. And what's all this about a holiday cottage and architects? That doesn't sound to me as if she's about to sell up and retire to sheltered accommodation.'

'Nor me,' Kerri agreed.

'Then why insist on us coming here?'

'You, not us.'

'She knows you're coming, too. I read your reply to her e-mail.'

'I've a feeling it's you she wants, not me. She's putting up with me as a bad job. I'm not so sure I like that.'

Damien laughed.

'It's your fighting spirit coming to the fore as always.'

She hit him hard with the back of her hand, spilled the rest of her coffee, gave an exclamation of dismay and sprang up.

'Now look what you made me do!' She pulled a tissue from her pocket and dabbed at the front of her jacket.

'Serve you right,' Damien said without moving.

She made the best job of it as she could, squeezed the stained tissues into a ball and thrust the tissue into her pocket. This wasn't the moment to reply to his taunts and start an argument.

They could hear the sound of voices now. Someone was coming, two people, and one of

16

them was Leo.

The girl walking jauntily along at Leo's side looked young and round-faced. Her sleeveless red T-shirt was bright against the grey building behind her.

She was smiling and gesticulating, then stopped abruptly on seeing them.

Kerri and Damien, standing side-by-side, stared.

'I've found her for you,' Leo said, looking pleased. 'Macey, your visitors!'

She gazed at Damien.

'Hi there, Damien. It's good to see you.'

Damien cleared his throat.

'And this is Kerri.'

'Kerri? Ah, your sister.'

'You're Eustacia Treghennel?' Kerri said, still hardly able to believe she wasn't the elderly lady they had imagined.

Eustacia giggled.

'Macey to my friends.'

'A pretty name,' Damien said.

'You think so?' She dimpled up at him. 'You've come such a long way, Damien. I appreciate that.'

He smiled but Kerri was suspicious. Were they here on the whim of a girl?

'Has Leo shown you round the place yet?' Macey said. 'Well, there's plenty of time for that once you've seen your accommodation. Shall we go?'

Kerri stepped forward.

17

'That won't be necessary, thank you. We've made our own arrangements for a couple of nights.'

'You have? But that's not right.'

'I thought we made that perfectly clear in our reply to your e-mail.' Kerri's words sounded more curt than she intended and for a moment Macey looked disconcerted.

'Where are you staying?' Leo asked. 'Back there in the corner cottage, where the road joins the track? I thought the Wainwrights were fully booked.'

'I felt sure you'd want to stay here in the house, Damien.' Macey frowned.

'We're in accommodation in Rawthwaite.' Kerri glanced at Damien and saw that he was finding it difficult to take his eyes from the bubbly girl.

His silence made Kerri uneasy. Was he regretting their decision to be independent?

'We need to talk, Damien,' Macey said in her lilting voice that Kerri was beginning to find irritating.

'Of course, Macey.'

'Leo will look after your sister, won't you, Leo?'

'If you say so.' Undismayed Leo moved towards the tray from where they had left it on the wall. 'I'll deal with this first. Kerri can come, too.'

'Leave it!' Macey's voice was sharp.

He didn't argue. Instead he smiled at Kerri.

18

'Like to take a closer look at the hide, then?'

'I'd love to.'

He led the way to a narrow gate in the dry-stone wall on the other side of the track, opened it and stood aside for her to pass through in front of him. They walked on spongy grass until they reached a bed of reeds.

'I hope it's not too soggy for you.'

Kerri smiled.

'Not to worry, though boots would be more suitable.'

'But not as elegant as those pretty shoes.'

'I wanted to look my best to meet Macey,' she said as she avoided a squelchy patch. 'If I'd turned up in my old gardening gear she might have had nothing to do with us.'

He grinned.

'You think not?'

'Who knows?'

It wasn't quite true, she thought. Damien would have scored a hit with Macey even if he'd been wearing that awful magenta Aran jersey Lucy knitted for him for their hiking trip in the Lake District last Easter.

Leo looked interested.

'So you like gardening?'

'It's my job. I've been working in a large nursery near Bristol.' Kerri was filled suddenly with sadness because something that had meant so much to her only a few days ago seemed already to have faded into the distant

19

past.

They neared the edge of the reservoir and paused.

'Here we are,' he said. 'What do you think of this mound of dead branches and heather?'

'Impressive,' she said.

The hide Leo indicated was half-shielded by a mass of hazel bushes and long grass and was almost invisible.

'It's been here long enough now to be accepted by the local wildlife,' he said. 'Keen birdwatchers can be sure of a good day's viewing if they get into position before dawn.'

He pulled aside some loose branches over the entrance and they went inside. It was roomy enough to hold several people. A long narrow gap in the wall of branches and dead heather facing the reservoir gave an excellent view of it and the land on the other side. There was even a makeshift bench inside.

They sat down and Leo pulled out a pair of folding binoculars from the pocket of his jeans. He focused them and swung them round in a wide arc and then back again.

'Nothing much at the moment.'

'Over there, to the right of that low tree?'

'Well spotted. An avocet . . . no, two of them. You've got sharp eyes.' He studied them for a minute or two and then passed the binoculars to her.

The avocets, elegantly white against their dull background, soon vanished into the

20

foliage.

'You have to be patient at this sort of game.'

'Do you do much of it?'

He shook his head.

'I'm too busy over at Alderbeck. I work at the adventure place there. We run courses and I tutor a bit. A local ornithologist takes care of all this.'

'What's your subject?'

'Horticulture, would you believe? We do all sorts of testing, of vegetables mostly. I love the research involved.' He moved his position a little on the bench.

'I've left some seeds soaking for an hour or two. Someone brought them back from somewhere exotic and we're seeing if we can grow them here.'

'Do you think you can?'

'It's the sort of challenge I like.'

She wished she could ask him about Macey and what the set-up here was all about and what part he played in it. But she couldn't do that without sounding impolite. He clearly had no idea why she and Damien were here either.

'And what sort of adventures are on offer?'

'All sorts of outdoor activities. You name it.'

'Sounds good.'

'Do you do anything else as well as garden, Kerri?'

She felt a shadow cross her face.

'Not really. Not lately. I used to like long-distance walking and swimming but there hasn't been much time for that.'

He nodded towards the gap in the hide.

'The water in the reservoir out there's a bit cold at the moment. I wouldn't advise diving in, though!'

She laughed.

'I'll pass. It looks less than inviting.'

'Sensible girl.' He laughed, too. 'There's plenty of good walking round here, though.' He snapped the binoculars shut. 'Seen enough here now for the moment? You'll have to come another day when there's more on offer.'

'We're not here for long,' she said. 'Tomorrow we'll be driving south. We have to get back because of Damien's work. And mine, too.'

Not only work in her case, she thought, reminded suddenly of André.

'That's a pity.' Leo sounded as if he really meant it.

Outside, the air was cooler as a bank of cloud slid across the sun. Tiny ripples disturbed the surface of the water.

'It's so peaceful here,' she said. 'I like it.'

'I'm glad.' His eyes half closed as he smiled at her.

'Did you know that Macey thinks we may be related?' she said in a rush.

'Related?' He looked at her quizzically.

'She told Damien she had proof.'

'And so that's why you're here?'

22

'She invited him.'

They returned to the house and found Macey and Damien in the kitchen at the back. The pleasant smell of coffee wafted across to them as they went in.

The wooden table in the middle of the room was covered with a sheet of paper the size of a doormat and Kerri saw that Damien had obviously been studying it.

He looked up as they went in.

'This is interesting, Kerri. Take a look.'

She could see it was some sort of family tree but before she could get close Macey pushed it to one side.

'Sit down and have some more coffee,' she said.

'Not for me,' Leo said. 'I've got things to do.'

She ignored him but he didn't seem to mind. He smiled at Kerri, raised his hand in salute to Damien and was off.

Kerri sat down while Macey busied herself pouring coffee into huge purple mugs with thick rims. She put some shortbread on a silver dish and placed it in front of Damien.

'Macey's been telling me how we fit in to her family tree,' he said.

'Our family tree,' Macey emphasised as she sat down close to Damien and bit into a piece of shortbread.

He smiled.

'The relationship's a bit distant but we're

23

there, sure enough. We share the same great-great-grandfather.'

'That's going back a bit.'

Damien considered.

'Late nineteenth century, I should think.'

'John Treghennel,' Macey said with satisfaction. A shortbread crumb fell on her T-shirt and she brushed it off. Her nail varnish wasn't the same shade of red as her shirt, but the disparity that on anyone else might have seemed a mistake, on Macey looked charming.

Kerri wished she could see the sheet of paper for herself. 'What relation are we to each other, then?'

'Distant cousins,' Macey said with a brilliant smile.

'Very distant by the sound of it.'

'But my only relatives.'

'What happened to all the others in the family tree?' Damien frowned.

'I wondered that, too.'

'Worry not,' Macey said gaily. 'They did a lot of dying in infancy in those days. Lucky for us, Damien, or we might not be together now.'

Kerri frowned. Together? She didn't like the tone of possessiveness in Macey's light-hearted words.

'Not all of them, surely?' she objected.

'They're not around now, anyway.'

'There were wars, too, don't forget,' Damien said.

Kerri thought of all the family members

24

who might well have lived between the days of her great-great-grandfather and today. They couldn't all have died in infancy, or been killed before they could marry and have children!

Macey gave Damien a playful tap on the shoulder. 'Enough of that. Drink up and I'll give you a grand tour.' She got up and folded the family tree with firmness. The walls in the downstairs rooms were as plain as the hall and there was no sign of family heirlooms of any sort. Kerri had expected antique furniture and portraits lining the walls but each room Macey showed them was devoid of anything that looked remotely old and just contained enough modern things to look comfortably lived-in.

'Upstairs now?' Macey's eyes danced.

Up here on the broad landing it was much the same. When she had shown them each of the six bedrooms and the huge bathroom Macey turned to Damien.

'Are you sure you're ready for this?'

He glanced swiftly at Kerri and she saw a flicker of excitement in his eyes.

Macey flicked a switch on the wall and as if by magic a trap door in the high ceiling opened and a folding ladder came slowly down.

She turned to look at them, her face alight with pleasure. 'My treasure trove,' she said. 'All stored away up there waiting to be unpacked and examined. Several days' work there, at least. I trust you are up for it,

Damien?'

There was a moment's silence. Then Damien smiled.

'I don't see why not,' he said.

## Secret Garden

Silenced by the speed at the way events were unfolding, Kerri could only look at her brother in dismay. Her plan to get Damien away from Cornwall and into a different environment had worked well, she thought. Far too well.

'That sounds a great idea,' Damien said, looking at her for confirmation. 'What do you think, Kerri?'

Taking a deep breath she said, 'I suppose staying one more day would be all right, if you're quite sure, Damien.'

She was hurt that he appeared so absorbed in Macey and the work planned for him that he gave no thought to her feelings. But his well-being was important to her, so how could she refuse him something that obviously meant so much, even if she was beginning to suspect Macey's motives for getting them here?

He smiled.

'I'm sure.'

Macey was still looking up at him, her head a little to one side. The dimple deepened in her right cheek.

'That's my Damien.'

A flicker of disquiet made Kerri's cheeks glow. She wondered that Damien wasn't aware of the trade he might be losing by staying longer than they planned. Roger, his assistant, was back from his holiday now and it was useful to have his help, but Damien was the expert. There were still some tourists about, the kind who liked to browse around antique shops at their leisure, picking things up to examine closely and hopefully buying. Damien should really be there.

'Right, then,' he said. 'Let's get going.'

Macey stood back while he examined the ladder, making sure it was safe, before climbing up and hauling himself through the gap in the ceiling. Kerri made a move to follow.

'I don't think so,' Macey said.

Kerri hesitated.

'Shouldn't we go up, too?'

'He knows what he needs to do.'

'But . . .'

'Are you all right up there, Damien?' Macey called.

'There's masses of stuff packed away in boxes.' His voice was muffled but Kerri could hear the excitement in it. 'Bigger things, too.'

Macey nodded unsmilingly at Kerri.

'He won't want us interfering.'

'Is there anything else I can do to help?'

'Take a look round outside, why don't you?'

27

Macey said in such an indifferent tone of voice that Kerri felt awkward.

'If that's what you want,' she said reluctantly.

Macey, gazing up into the gap, didn't answer. Kerri wondered if, as soon as her back was turned, she would be up there, too. But somehow she didn't think so. There had been a surprisingly defenceless look about Macey when she stepped back from the ladder, as if she were afraid of going up there but didn't want to admit it.

Kerri shrugged and turned away. Outside, the shadows from the trees threw deep patterns on the cobbled yard at the side of the house and the air was warm. She went through a gate in the wall and found herself in a large expanse of waste ground stretching uphill and bounded on four sides by high stone walls. A walled garden? It seemed like it, although in its overgrown state it was hard to imagine. What a wonderful space! If it were hers she would fill it with scent and colour and grow shrubs and flowers to attract butterflies.

She clanged the gate shut behind her and went farther on. Up in the far corner a couple of ancient apple trees almost hid a ruined building that looked like a shed. She could see now that the tangle of weeds and brambles in some places weren't as thick as she had thought at first glance.

She set to work, pulling them clear and

28

unearthing a way up the central path that she soon saw was crossed by another half way up. This was the kind of physical work she liked, heaving away at things to improve the surroundings and make sense out of what plainly had once been a thriving garden.

After a while she stopped for a rest, panting a little, and looked back at the roof of the house just visible above the wall. An array of chimneys made an interesting pattern against the sky.

Then she turned back to her self-imposed task. By the time she reached the top of the garden she was exhausted. She was pleased to see that the shed wasn't as dilapidated as it had looked from below, even though the door stood loose on its hinges and one of the smeared windows was broken.

Inside, it was empty apart from a couple of folded wooden chairs covered in dust and cobwebs. Pulling one of them outside, she cleaned it off as well as she could and sat down gingerly in case it collapsed under her weight.

The sunshine was pleasant and for a few moments she closed her eyes, enjoying the warmth on her face and the scent of mint and thyme from somewhere close by. The ground that had been disturbed on one side of the path smelled moist and earthy. Insects buzzed near at hand and further afield she heard the sound of a car engine.

She wished she had a garden of her own

to plant out as she wished and to enjoy on summer evenings. André was so brilliant at knowing what was needed to make Roseleaf a success that it didn't occur to him that she might like to plan and experiment on her own sometimes. But, of course, that wouldn't do in a commercial enterprise like Roseleaf.

The latch on the gate down below rattled and Kerri opened her eyes to see a figure coming up the path towards her, leaping across the wrenched-out weeds and reaching her in seconds.

'Hi, there, Kerri.' Leo flicked back the hair that fell over his forehead. 'Enjoying the sunshine?'

She sat upright and smiled.

'The view's not bad from here either,' she said.

He laughed.

'Mind if I join you?' He reached inside the shed for the other chair, rubbed off the cobwebs and sat down too.

'How were the seeds?'

'Alive and kicking. All planted in seedboxes now and in the propagator.'

'I was planning what I'd do with the garden if I had one like this.'

He screwed up his eyes as he regarded the scene in front of them.

'The whole place needs clearing. I'd get the digger in and start afresh.'

'Not check what's growing there beneath all

that foliage first?'

'Very little, I should think. The place hadn't been touched for years before Macey moved in and she's no gardener.'

'She inherited the property?'

He nodded.

'From her grandfather. Sadly no money came with it to run it properly. There wasn't any, I suppose, only those boxes of treasures of hers. Maybe they'll bring her in a fortune, who knows? I wouldn't have the first idea.'

Damien would, Kerri thought. How lucky for Macey that this was Damien's line of work. He would know instantly whether or not they contained anything whose value would make a huge difference to her.

'She must have been devastated when her grandfather died, if he was her only close relation.'

Leo shrugged.

'I don't suppose she knew him. He lived here as a recluse. I never knew much about him when I was growing up in Alderfield.'

'That's the place back there at the head of the reservoir?' He nodded.

'I don't think he ever had much to do with his family.'

'That's sad.'

'Dad knew him slightly and my parents have moved away now. That's why Dad asked me to keep an eye on Macey, and to call in when I can. It was a surprise to everyone when she

31

moved in.'

'I can imagine.'

'She knows that it's far too big a place for her to cope with without suitable finance, of course. Fitting out the holiday cottage was a crazy idea from the start. She's been advised to put both on the market and get something smaller but she's still reluctant to do it.'

'So finding a fortune could make a difference?'

'Maybe.'

Kerri would like to have asked more about Macey but now wasn't the time. Instead she said 'So, how would you set about making the most of this space?'

His eyes lit up.

'Planning first, of course, on the drawing board.'

'I love delphiniums. I'd have a long border of them in the distance where I'd see them when I opened the door at the bottom.' She gazed dreamily across the tangled space imagining it flowering and producing in all its glory.

'Several greenhouses,' he said. 'And propagating sheds. A large paved area for storage, sheds . .

'Roses rambling over arches and a pergola covered in purple wisteria.'

'You're not serious?' Leo said, leaning forward. 'Such a waste. A paradise for experiments, that's how I see it.'

'We don't seem to be agreeing on anything here.'

He laughed.

'Just as well Macey isn't employing the pair of us as a team of garden designers then. Practical, that's my middle name. I'd make a go of this my way if I had the chance.'

'Does Macey know that?'

'She takes my advice on many other things but not on the garden.'

'And yet that's your expertise.'

'In any case she's been deeply involved in renovating the cottage into holiday accommodation and I'm glad to help her with that. Dad was a builder and I picked up a thing or two along the way.'

'Useful.'

Leo nodded.

'You could say that. I'm only too glad to help.'

Kerri thought of Macey and how she'd got Damien sorting through her treasures for her.

'I could show you some of the work I'm doing over at Alderbeck if you're interested,' Leo said.

'I'd like that.'

'Now?'

'Why not? I don't seem to be needed here at the moment.'

He got up.

'We'll check what's going on first.' With one smooth movement he folded his chair

33

and reached for hers and put them back in the shed. Then he paused to examine the door that was hanging open on its hinges. 'I'll take a look at this later and do something about it,' he said. 'The broken window, too.'

Kerri followed him down the path, stepping carefully over the piles of undergrowth she had pulled up earlier. The time had passed pleasantly in Leo's company and she saw that it was past twelve o'clock as they walked across the yard. The kitchen was empty and so was the hall. The huge front door stood wide open and outside she glimpsed a table and chairs.

Macey got up from one of them and came forward smiling.

'Damien's just coming. We're eating lunch out here.'

A large loaf was on the breadboard in the middle of the table with a bowl of salad nearby. A butter dish, cheese board and a bowl of fruit took up the rest of the space.

Leo pulled out one of the spare chairs for Kerri and sat down himself.

'You've done us proud, Macey,' he said.

She shot him a conspiratorial glance that seemed to exclude Kerri so that for a moment she wondered what she was doing here. But there were four place-settings at the table and the sun was warm on her face. Being unduly sensitive wasn't usually one of her failings so what was the matter with her today?

When Damien took his place by Macey

34

Kerri saw that his hair was grey with dust. He looked tired but happy.

'So how did it go, Damien?' she asked.

'Plenty to do yet,' Macey answered for him.

Leo helped himself to a piece of bread and spread butter on it.

'And Kerri's surplus to requirements?'

'Kerri?' Macey said. She frowned. 'Oh, yes, Kerri. I'd forgotten her for a moment.'

'Just as well someone hasn't,' Leo said. 'I'm carrying her off to Alderbeck this afternoon to inspect the place and to see what I busy myself doing there.'

'But I might need you here,' Macey said.

Leo smiled. He seemed unperturbed by any plans she might have for him as he stood up to cut more bread and handed it round.

'Doing what?' he said easily. 'It seems you'll be fully occupied with all your plans for the afternoon. You know I'll be back when I'm needed here.'

Expecting Macey to insist, Kerri said nothing. She could always spend time in the garden behind the house again and amuse herself there until it was time to return to Rawthwaite. And then tomorrow they would be off on the long drive to Cornwall and she need never see the place again. She felt a stirring of disappointment at the thought that surprised her.

But Macey laughed.

'Of course, Leo. I'd forgotten what we

35

agreed.'

Damien seemed too tired to talk and the others ate in silence, too. After all the fresh air Kerri began to feel drowsy.

Leo finished eating and sprang up.

'We'll be off then,' he said. 'Get a move on, Kerri.'

'But . . .'

'No arguments.'

He ushered her through the gate and towards his vehicle. As he drove off he grinned.

'We've a long afternoon ahead of us if I show you everything.'

'But the clearing up here . . .?'

'Can be done later. Or not at all.'

Macey would need something to do while Damien was hard at it up in the loft, Kerri thought. With luck all the boxes could be down by the time they got back and then Macey would have time, with Damien's help and perhaps her own, to sort through them to find what she was looking for.

She leaned back in her seat and smiled.


## Talking To Lucy

They drove back alongside the reservoir and through the group of grey-roofed houses that made up the hamlet of Alderfield out on to the main road and then south towards Rawthwaite. After a mile or two they turned right along a narrow lane Kerri hadn't noticed when they passed that way this morning.

Alderbeck House was a large building of weathered stone standing back behind a wide expanse of lawn bounded on each side by trees and shrubs. As they drove through the open gates Kerri caught sight of a church tower on the left behind the trees. They parked at the back of the house.

'This is impressive,' Kerri said as she got out and stared up at the building.

Leo smiled.

'Wait till you see inside.'

They entered through a small side door that led into a narrow passage that took them into a large tiled hallway. Here the walls were papered with a cheerful design of summer flowers. Alderbeck House had obviously been a private home once and still retained an atmosphere of cosiness and welcome Kerri found pleasant. She liked the faint scent of lavender, too.

'This way,' Leo said indicating that she should follow him.

There were sounds of activity in the downstairs rooms they passed to reach a larger one at the front of the house. Leo opened the door and ushered Kerri inside. Here there were easy chairs and overflowing bookcases as well as a TV set in the corner. Beneath her feet the sisal floor covering felt unyielding but was obviously hard-wearing and practical.

'This is the reception area,' Leo said. 'And somewhere to relax in the evenings too. We think of everything. Have you noticed this?'

Kerri now saw that in an alcove camouflaged by a cabinet at the far end was a drinks machine.

Leo grinned.

'Shall I demonstrate? Coffee OK? Take a seat, Kerri.'

She did as he said and found one with a view of the front drive and the trees beyond.

He brought two cups of coffee and placed them on the low table in front of them.

'I'll show you my office and lecture room in a minute. I think you'll be impressed. They built on an extension last year with a heated greenhouse attached and easy access to the garden, and there I spend a lot of my time.'

'But not today?' she said.

'My next group arrives next week,' he said. 'And since I'm up to date with a plan of action for them I took the day off.'

'You're allowed to do that?'

'Of course. I make my own agenda.'

'Sounds good.'

'It's the way I like it.' He picked up his cup, tested it and put it down again. 'So, Kerri, you and Damien are brother and sister, I believe?'

'Twins, but we're not a bit alike. Damien's so like Dad as a young man it isn't true. I'm

38

more like our mother.'

'She must be beautiful.'

Kerri flushed.

'She was. I remember that. She died when we were young.'

'That's terrible.'

'Dad was father and mother to us.'

'And still is?'

She shook her head.

'Damien and I are on our own now. But we've got each other.' She picked up her cup and took a sip.

'Tell me, Kerri, what nursery garden did you say you worked at? Near Bristol, you said?'

'Roseleaf at Birchford. Do you know the place?'

He pulled out a notebook and Biro.

'Better make a note of that or I might forget as it's not familiar. So who's your boss?'

She hesitated, stabbed suddenly by the thought of André returning home to the news she had for him. It was even hard to get his name out and she stuttered over it a little.

'It's, well, André Simpson. At least . . . yes, André.'

Leo frowned as he wrote it down.

'You're sure about that?'

'Of course I'm sure,' she said indignantly.

She would soon be telling André she could no longer work there and must leave. But where would she go? She hadn't thought of that.

'I'll be able to check that on the internet, of course,' Leo said.

'Check?

'Macey needs to know, you see.'

'She does?'

Kerri had begun to think that she was invisible as far as Macey was concerned but she wasn't sure she liked the way this was going.

'And about your brother, too, of course. How long has he been running his business?'

'His business?'

Leo looked up at the incredulous tone in Kerri's voice. Damien had said nothing about the antiques gallery to Macey. She was sure of that because she had asked him as they travelled north, and her brother wouldn't lie to her.

'You don't mind my questions?' Leo looked anxious. 'Nothing personal. Just routine. Macey needs to know these things, you see. She has to be sure you're genuine.'

'And she asked you to find out?'

'This seemed a good opportunity. That's why she asked me to take it on.'

Kerri stared down at her cup. She could understand this on one level, of course, but Leo had seemed so friendly in inviting her here this afternoon that she had assumed he liked her and wanted her company for her own sake.

But it wasn't like that at all. He was

following Macey's orders and was probably bored with the job already. It would get her out of the way at Alder Knowle, too, and that's what Macey had made plain that she wanted. 'Nothing personal,' Leo had said and that hurt.

Leo smiled.

'Drink up and I'll show you my domain.'

Kerri tried to summon her enthusiasm as she viewed the lecture room at the back of the house but she was thinking all the time that she was here on sufferance to be got out of the way. Of course their credentials must be checked so why did she mind so much that it was Leo doing it?

He opened a wide shallow drawer in a unit beneath the window.

'This is where I keep the print-outs of the test records.'

Kerri leaned forward to look.

'Such fine detail.'

'I enjoy the recording almost as much as the practical work. We do tests for soil suitability and different altitudes.'

'You harvest your own seeds?'

He nodded.

'That's one of the subjects of the course next week. And propagating, of course. Come, I'll show you my space outside.'

She smiled. He was so enthusiastic about his work that she began to enjoy herself after all and was glad to be here in his company.

He opened a gate in the wall at the side of

the house. Here was a garden much smaller than she had anticipated. She gazed at the straight lines and sharp angles of the raised beds, the neat rows marked out by bamboo canes.

'It's beautifully flat,' she said.

He looked at it with pride.

'My own domain. Exactly how I like it.'

Kerri moved among the beds while Leo told her how he worked the trials of different species of each vegetable.

'I'm planning a book,' he said. 'I think I've found a gap in the market so it seems a good idea. It makes sense of all I've been doing since I got here and several people seem to approve of the idea. The problem of course, is time.'

'It seems a great life doing what you want,' Kerri said.

'Frustrating sometimes. I'd like more space.'

To fill with more testing ground, more symmetry, she thought. A little depressing when it could be filled with the rampant colour of flowers creating beauty wherever you looked. Even Roseleaf had its areas where colour predominated.

At last she looked at her watch.

'I'd better get back,' she said reluctantly. 'Our evening meal's at seven and we mustn't miss it. They'll be expecting us and might worry. It's later than I thought.'

On the return journey they talked of

gardens they had visited in the past and of things they had learned and they were back at Macey's place far sooner than seemed possible.

Damien and Macey were sitting together at the kitchen table and were deep in conversation when Kerri found them.

Macey looked up expectantly.

'Where's Leo?'

'He dropped me off,' Kerri said feeling somehow in the wrong.

'But I need him here.' Macey leaped up and made for the door. They heard the front door slam after her and then silence. A few minutes later she was back and threw herself down in her seat again.

'Everything all right?' Damien asked.

Macey stretched both arms above her head and then got up again.

'I must have my shower now and be ready for Leo. We've an exciting evening ahead of us. Oh, yes, he insisted on that, tired as he is after a gruelling afternoon. See you tomorrow then, Damien.'

It sounded like a dismissal but even so they didn't get away for another half hour because Macey had something she wanted to show Damien that she had forgotten about before. Feeling frustrated Kerri waited outside where she could look down over the calm water of the reservoir.

Damien seemed too tired to talk as Kerri

43

drove along the road she was beginning to know well. She wondered exactly where in the cluster of houses that made up Alderfield Leo had been born and spent his childhood. It was a great place to grow up, she thought.

As they drove down the Rawthwaite road on the other side of the water Kerri's mobile alerted her to a message.

'Do you mind Damien?' she said as she pulled into a lay-by. 'I've obviously picked up a signal here and it might be a voicemail message André sent earlier.'

It was. She got out of the car and opened the message, feeling disloyal because Leo had been filling her thoughts since they set off. After the message ended she stood for a moment, gazing across the calm water. She had felt sad hearing André's deep voice, totally unsuspicious of how she now felt about him. Suddenly she grabbed a tissue from her pocket. She took several deep breaths until she felt better.

She got back into the car.

'What does he say?' Damien asked slumped in the seat beside her. 'You didn't tell him?'

She didn't answer for a moment but concentrated on sending a text message.

'André wants me to check on one of the greenhouses,' she said. 'That's all. He didn't even know we're up here because I'd forgotten to tell him.'

'A different problem, then.'

'I'll phone Carol from Rawthwaite and get her to go in and do it for me.'

Kerri switched on the ignition and they set off again. She would contact André again later and explain what had been happening.

There was very little parking in front of the terraced house where they were staying but Kerri just managed to squeeze the car into a small space.

As it turned out they were only just in time too to book in for another night, because a family from Norwich was coming after that and the accommodation was all taken.

'That should do us nicely,' Kerri said when they got up from the dinner table.

One more day under Macey's orders would be quite enough, she thought.

'I've eaten too much.' Damien yawned as they left the room. 'I am shattered. I'll have an early night, I think. You don't mind, do you? See you in the morning.'

He would be raring to get back to Alder Knowle, Kerri thought, dispirited. She went to the window but all she could see were the grey-stone cottages opposite.

There was nothing she wanted to see on TV. The book she had brought with her was in her room and she would be better off there, too.

The view was nicer up here because she had a glimpse of hills as well as buildings. She threw herself down on the bed and got out her mobile.

45

She pressed André's name on her list of contacts and heard the ringing tone in far-away Switzerland. No answer. She left a message and then lay back on her bed.

She thought of Lucy, picked up the phone again and clicked on Lucy's number.

'Hello?' Lucy's clear voice sounded uncertain.

'Lucy . . .' Kerri began.

'Kerri! Is everything OK?'

'I miss you.' Kerri spoke breathlessly.

'Me, too.'

'There's so much to tell you.'

'Where are you?'

'Damien and I drove north yesterday, to the Dales.' Kerri hadn't meant to mention her brother's name but there was no way it could be avoided.

'I wish it didn't have to be like this between us.' Lucy's voice was wistful.

'I know,' she said. 'It's difficult. I don't want things to change between us because of what happened.'

'We won't let it.' Lucy's voice was stronger now. 'I want to hear everything you've been doing, Kerri.'

Kerri settled back against the pillow and let it all come pouring out without dwelling too much on Damien.

'I'll be helping out tomorrow, and then we'll be driving south on Tuesday,' she said.

When the call ended Kerri was smiling. She

46

and Lucy had made proper contact and would do so again.

*     *     *

Kerri had had a quick look round the town by the time Damien put in an appearance at the breakfast table. There were dark shadows beneath his eyes.

'You OK, Damien?' she asked.

He nodded as he reached for the jug of orange juice.

'A heavy day yesterday, that's all.'

Damien had appeared to have forgotten the trauma of the last few days in his surprise that Eustacia had turned into young and vibrant Macey, needing his help with the sorting out of boxes of antiques for her.

And valuing them? Kerri paused with her cereal spoon halfway to her mouth. Could it be that Macey knew what she was doing, and this was a cheap way of getting everything valued?

Damien looked at her sharply.

'What's wrong?'

'Nothing,' she said, just as she used to when growing up and she wanted to hide something from him. After all, what did it matter? Once this was over they would be able to head south. She thought briefly of Leo. Meeting him had been a pleasant interlude in all this, but that was all.

Once on the road again Kerri tried to put

47

her suspicions about Macey's motives from her mind.

'So what was Macey so keen to show you before we left her yesterday?'

'Nothing much,' Damien said. 'Just to tell me the plans for today. We've most of the boxes down on the landing, as you know. We'll get the rest down this morning, to make it easier to unpack the contents and then go through them carefully in case there is anything of real value there.'

'Which you would recognise, naturally.'

'I hope so.'

Kerri chose her words.

'Macey knew the right person to invite up here, then.'

'Can you blame her?'

'You're aware of it?' she said in surprise.

'I didn't want you flying off the handle if I told you.'

'When did you find out?'

'Before we left yesterday. She told me so herself.'

'So there was more than you let on?'

Kerri felt hurt when he didn't answer. Damien didn't often hide anything from her. But she had worked this out for herself, so shouldn't she be pleased that Macey was open and honest about it? And to be fair, she had promised that she would be giving Damien some of the inherited possessions she thought should be passed on to someone with the same

48

family connections.

'It'll take some time to sort through everything,' Damien said at last.

'Can I help with that?'

'Why not?' He sounded surprised.

'Macey might have other plans for me.'

'Do I detect a hint of bitterness there?'

'I could have helped you lift those boxes down yesterday.'

'And missed an afternoon of garden chat?'

'There is that,' Kerri said.

If she were honest she had enjoyed herself at Alderbeck. Leo was such good company and the time had flown.

She felt Damien come alive suddenly as they turned off the main road and drove through the village of Alderfield to turn right again down the track to Alder Knowle.

'Almost too good a day to spend indoors,' he said.

'Don't let Macey hear you say that.'

He laughed.

'Am I forgiven then?'

She smiled.

'Poor Macey.'

'Why is that?'

'No family. Only us.'

'Lucky Macey, then.'

'Lucky Macey, then,' she repeated.

# The Estate Agent

Macey was waiting for them at the front door, dressed today in jeans and a yellow shirt with her dark hair pulled back from her face by a red band. She didn't smile as they approached, but looked anxious.

'I was afraid you wouldn't come back,' Macey said.

Damien grinned.

'No danger of that.'

It was strange seeing Macey's vulnerability when yesterday she had seemed full of confidence, and Kerri felt a stirring of sympathy for her.

'Come on, then,' Macey said.

They went inside.

'Coffee? I've just made some,' Macey said.

'I'd rather get straight on with things, if you don't mind, Macey. We're off tomorrow and I'd like to get finished. I'll make a start, shall I, while you two girls have yours?' Without waiting for an answer he was off up the stairs. Macey poured the coffee.

'I was expecting Leo here before now,' she said.

Kerri's heart gave a little lurch.

'Leo's coming?'

'He said he would.'

'It's early yet.'

'I phoned,' Macey insisted. 'There was no answer.'

'Then he must be on his way.'

Macey looked unconvinced but sat up straighter now. 'We've got a busy day in front of us.'

'So Damien said.'

'There might not be anything valuable in the boxes.'

'You don't know?'

Macey shrugged.

'How could I? They were in the loft when I moved in.'

'But they could be full of treasure, for all you know.'

'We'll soon see. Do you know about antiques?'

'Dad used to take us to antiques fairs with him sometimes,' she said. 'I used to try and get out of it but somehow managed to pick up the odd bit of know-how.'

'You're lucky to have a father like that.'

'Not any more.'

'He died? And your mother? Mine, too, a long time ago.'

'Who brought you up?'

Macey had a closed expression on her face.

'I don't talk about it.'

Sorry she had asked, Kerri sipped her coffee in silence. Macey leaped up.

'I'm off. You can tell Damien. Things to do.'

Kerri heard a car start up and drive off.

51

She stayed where she was to finish her coffee and then washed both mugs at the sink and left them to drain. There was a ring at the doorbell.

Outside stood a tall young man in a pink jacket whose wispy hair hung down over the collar. He smiled.

'Miss Treghennel?'

Surprised Kerri nodded before realising it was Macey he meant.

'I'm here about the property,' he said before she could explain her mistake. 'We tried to phone and when we couldn't get through I thought it best to come straight away and get some details. Our client is in a hurry, you see.'

'You couldn't get through?'

'A fault somewhere. You'll need to report it.'

'There's no signal for my mobile.'

'I will do it when I get back. Anyway . . .?'

'But I'm not Miss Treghennel.' She flushed. 'Not the one you want, I mean. She has just gone out, I'm afraid.'

'No matter. I take it you could show me round?' He had a card out at once and held it out to her. 'My credentials.'

She shook her head as she took it from him.

'Sorry. I have not got the authority to do that.'

He looked annoyed.

'Then I've wasted my time?'

'I'll get her to contact you as soon as she

52

gets back.'

For a second she thought he wouldn't go but then he seemed to make up his mind suddenly. She watched him drive slowly away and hoped she had done the right thing.

By the time Macey returned ten minutes later, Kerri had checked that Damien, up in the depths of the loft, didn't need any assistance from her.

'I'll give you a shout when I do,' he called.

From her viewpoint at the top of the loft ladder she could see she wasn't needed and climbed down again quickly as she heard the front door crash shut.

She met Macey in the hall.

'Someone called,' Kerri told her. 'An estate agent.'

'Oh?'

'He said he had an appointment.' Kerri felt for the card in the pocket of her jeans. 'I said you would phone when you got back. He couldn't get through on the phone.'

'Of course he couldn't,' Macey snapped. 'I gave him the wrong number.'

Kerri looked at her and was surprised to see tears welling up in Macey's eyes. She knew better than to comment as she followed her into the kitchen.

Macey dropped the bag she was carrying onto the floor and thumped herself down at the table.

'A problem?' Kerri ventured.

53

'You could say that.' Macey's lips trembled. 'I saw Leo. On his way out of his house. He's not coming.'

Kerri's shiver of disappointment was ridiculous but she couldn't help it. She sat down opposite Macey.

'Can I do anything?'

Macey buried her face in her hands.

'He said he had things to do that were important.'

'Couldn't that be true?'

'He wouldn't have said that . . . once. He would have been here with me. What could be more important?'

Kerri bit back a smile.

'He said he will come tomorrow instead,' Macey said.

'That's good.' Kerri hoped she didn't sound disheartened but it meant she wouldn't see Leo again and somehow that mattered a lot.

'He doesn't like me any more,' Macey said dolefully.

'You don't know that. He hasn't said so, has he?'

Macey looked at her hopefully.

'No. You think he still does?'

Kerri nodded. To her relief she heard a shout from above.

'That's Damien.' She jumped up. 'He said he would call when he was ready for some help.'

Immediately Macey brightened.

54

'Damien needs me!'

She raced up the stairs ahead of Kerri, her dark hair swinging from its red band.

'I'm here, Damien. I'm coming!'

He had manoeuvred four wooden boxes to the top of the loft ladder and needed help in getting them down safely.

'They are heavy,' he warned.

It took time but at last they had placed them next to the others on the landing.

With some difficulty the three of them broke open the first of them and removed the contents. Kerri could see that there was nothing here of much value among the dishes and vegetable bowls and the odd pair of silver-plated candlesticks that were chipped and uncared for.

'All rubbish,' Macey said discouraged.

Kerri sat back on her heels, hoping that all the boxes weren't the same.

'We'd better get this lot downstairs out of the way,' Damien said cheerfully. 'There are plenty more boxes where these came from.'

He helped her struggle downstairs with it.

The next box contained some bookends made of alabaster which looked in good condition. Damien lifted them out carefully and placed them on the floor near Macey.

'These might be worth something,' he said. 'They're an attractive design. Worth a try.'

'You think so?' Macey looked hopeful.

Damien was already opening the next

55

box. Kerri and Macey crowded round as he wrenched the lid off to reveal the contents packed tightly together. As each item was unpacked Kerri had no idea what most of them were.

'It will take ages to get them all out,' Macey said. 'Can't we just tip the lot out on the floor?'

'No way,' Damien said with authority. 'Careful now. We don't want any breakages.'

Macey smiled at him.

'You're so masterful, Damien. I like that.'

He didn't appear to hear but Kerri recognised a telltale flush beneath his jaw bone. To create a diversion, she pretended to drop the glass dish she was holding.

'Now who is careless?' Macey moved closer to Damien.

After an hour Kerri had had enough. She wondered that her brother didn't ask Macey to give him more space. Instead he appeared to be enjoying her closeness.

She got to her feet and stretched.

'Sorry to break up the party. But we'll have to do something about lunch. Do you want me to go and book us in somewhere, Macey? Somewhere not too far away.'

'Is it that time already?' Damien was looking at his watch now and beginning to make a move to stop work.

'Stay where you are,' Macey commanded. 'I'm well stocked with food here. No need to go anywhere.'

'But we can't . . .' Kerri began.

'Find something for us, will you? Shout when it's ready.'

'Damien?' Kerri said uncertainly.

'Thanks, Macey. That's great.' He smiled.

Kerri could hardly refuse but as she went downstairs she was smarting.

The afternoon was almost over when Macey gazed at the mountain of items they had been busy unpacking. Damien had made a start on dividing them into sections, but as time progressed he became more interested in each individual item and was loath to put it down again.

'How valuable is it?' Macey asked each time, hopeful.

Damien placed each piece carefully on the floor.

'I can't say until I've done a bit of research. But don't get your hopes up too high, Macey.'

'When can you do that?'

'When I get access to a computer. I didn't bring my laptop, you see.'

Macey's face fell and then lit up again.

'I'll get Leo to bring his over.' She sprang up from where she was kneeling. 'My computer's on the blink.'

She rushed down the stairs. Kerri listened to her excited voice on the telephone in the hall, knowing this provided the perfect excuse for her to get Leo to come.

But she came slowly back up the stairs.

57

'He'll drop it in later. He has plans for the evening but he is happy to leave it here and he'll pick it up tomorrow.'

'That's good then, isn't it?' Damien said.

Macey didn't answer.

Unaware of anything wrong Damien continued to examine each piece, making no effort to hurry.

'We'll never be finished at this rate,' Kerri warned.

Taking the empty boxes downstairs was her self-imposed task. As she returned from stacking another in the outhouse she heard the low murmur of voices.

'I'll do that, then,' Macey said, smiling as she passed Kerri on the stairs.

Kerri looked after her suspiciously.

'She's phoning for take-aways,' Damien told her.

Kerri sighed.

Damien was gazing down at an ugly china figure in his hand. He ran his fingers over the body.

'Look at this, Kerri. It's beautiful.' He looked up at her, his face shining. 'There might be more. And some of them might have some value. But not this chap, I'm afraid.'

Kerri looked dispiritedly at the boxes.

'How long is all this going to take?'

He shrugged.

'Another few days.'

'But what about the shop?'

58

'Roger's there, don't forget.' He looked at her. 'We're needed here, Kerri.'

'You're needed at the shop, too.'

He was silent and she didn't press it.

'Where will we stay?'

'The holiday cottage is more or less ready.'

'But we can't just move in there.'

'Macey's already suggested it. She really needs our help,' Damien said, looking his most persuasive. 'You can see how she's placed Kerri. We need to stay on for a bit.'

Kerri gazed at her brother in dismay.

'André is back on Thursday. I must be there, too.'

She heard footsteps on the stairs. Macey ran up towards them, smiling.

'Leo's just brought his laptop,' she said. 'And the order is in. Chinese all right for you?'

After they had eaten Kerri went outside. She left Damien at the cleared kitchen table focusing on the laptop with Macey standing behind him and breathing down his neck.

The air felt pleasantly cool on Kerri's face after the warmth of the kitchen. She hadn't been hungry and had merely toyed with the variety of dishes spread out on the kitchen table. She needed time to come to terms with Damien's infatuation for Macey. The sooner they were out of here the better.

Kerri breathed deeply, aware she could do nothing about the situation until it had run its course. Damien would ignore anything she said, even though he might be making the mistake of his life. The whole thing was ridiculous.

Kerri shrugged in frustration and then started to climb up the hill behind the house, feeling the need to be somewhere away from the others for a while. She had always liked high places and seeing into the far distance. When she was growing up it had been over the sea, and now she needed to gaze over countryside and give her thoughts full rein. She had another reason, too. From the summit she was likely to get a signal on her phone.

She climbed steadily up through the dying heather stalks and swathes of dull grass, thinking of Lucy. This time last year Lucy and Damien had been a couple and André has just asked her to marry him. Now all that had changed and André was still in ignorance of her change of heart. She wished she had been able to tell him right away. She would as soon as she could confront André when he was home.

So what was stopping her being there? Unbidden, the thought of Leo came into her mind and she gazed down over the waters of the reservoir and tried not to think of the happiness that flooded her when they were together.

Damien was determined to stay here and continue to help Macey but it didn't mean she had to. She had thought that Macey was making a play for Damien. But Macey's reaction to Leo's absence this morning suggested something different. If so, she could safely leave her brother here for a day or two while she drove back to Bristol. André was due back on Thursday afternoon. She would then tell him of the decision she had made about the future.

Kerri sat down on a bank of dry grass. She hated to hurt André but it had to be done, even though the dread of driving back for that purpose was a heavy load on her heart.

But maybe she wasn't being completely honest with herself in being reluctant to leave here. Didn't her growing attraction to Leo come into the equation, too?

She leaned forward and picked a piece of heather stem. She mustn't think of Leo but must concentrate on doing the right thing. She could get the bulk of her packing done when she got down to Bristol tomorrow evening, and then load her car. After that she dare not think. All she knew was that she would head north again after it was over, and put as much distance between herself and André as she could. She might even spend the night with Lucy and come on to Alder Knowle next day. Damien would need a lift back to Cornwall to transport the items Macey had promised him.

The late sunshine was warmer to her now and the visibility improved. From the top of the hill the bird hide down below was invisible, but she knew exactly where it was because Leo had shown her. She mustn't think of Leo any more. That way lay unhappiness.

She pulled out her mobile to click on Lucy's number, then she paused. Her friend might be in the middle of a lesson and not free to talk. A text message would have to do for now with the promise to speak later.

One more night in Rawthwaite, Kerri thought with resolution, back here once more tomorrow to drop off Damien, and then she would head south.


## An Accident

Next morning, as they drove along the lane after leaving the main road Damien let out a shout of warning. An approaching vehicle was coming at them at speed in the middle of the road. Almost too late it swerved. Kerri did too and pulled up, shaking, at the side of the road.

Damien was out at once and staring after the offending car as it vanished round the bend.

'He came at us so fast!' She felt dizzy with the shock it of it all and her hands were trembling.

'He could have had us in the ditch!' Damien looked at her in concern. 'Are you OK, Kerri? Here, let me drive.'

'I'll be all right in a minute.' She took a deep breath, aware suddenly of pain in her left hand. 'I must have knocked my hand. It hurts.'

'Let me see.'

She held it out to him and winced as he touched it.

'Do you think you've broken it?'

'It'll be all right in a minute.' She tried to waggle her fingers. 'It's the ball of the thumb that's beginning to swell.'

'We're almost at the turning to Macey's place,' Damien said. 'It's a private road. It'll be OK for me to drive.'

Reluctantly Kerri opened the car door and got out. She walked round and then slipped into the passenger seat.

'The sooner we get you there the better,' Damien said.

They had left Rawthwaite early to allow plenty of time but she hadn't bargained for this. As the engine came to life she leaned back and closed her eyes, reliving the moment when the other car had come at them.

By the time they reached the bridge and parked by the wall Kerri had stopped trembling. Macey came running down the path to meet them as they got out of the car. She smiled at Damien, tossing back her dark hair that had escaped from its peacock-blue band.

'You're later than I thought.'

'We had a bit of an incident with another vehicle back there.'

Macey looked at him, shocked.

'You're not injured, Damien?'

He shook his head.

'Some idiot came at us and nearly knocked us off the road. Only Kerri's swift reaction stopped that.'

Macey frowned.

'That's all right, then.'

'Not quite. Kerri's a bit shaken.'

'I've hurt my hand. I knocked it on the dashboard.'

Macey glanced at her and then back to Damien.

'Leo's here already.'

'Ready to help?'

She looked disconsolate.

'Just off to town. He called in for his laptop first.'

Kerri flopped down on the wall. Her left hand felt peculiar and very painful.

Damien was sympathetic.

'Try flexing your fingers again.'

Kerri tried, relieved that she could move them.

'No bones broken,' Macey said.

'She needs to rest it a bit. Any coffee going?'

'Go on through.'

Leo was standing at the sink and swung round as he heard the kitchen door open.

'Hi, there! This is a nice surprise, seeing you again.' He reached for the coffee pot. 'Like some? I thought you'd have been off by now.'

64

'It didn't quite work out.'

He looked at her closely.

'Are you all right? You look pale. Here, sit down.'

She sank thankfully on to the chair.

He reached a mug down from the shelf.

'Sugar? No, you don't, do you? So, what's up?'

'A problem with a driver who took the bend too fast.'

He sat down and looked so full of concern that tears sprang to Kerri's eyes. She wiped them away hastily.

'You've a long drive ahead of you,' he said at last.

She nodded.

'Thanks for the coffee. I feel much better now.' She tried to stand up, found she couldn't and sat down again. 'Could you call Damien for me, so I can tell him I'll soon be off.'

'No,' Leo said without moving. 'You're in no fit state to get behind that wheel. You've hurt your hand badly.'

'But I have to go. Later, anyway, when I can manage it.'

'Would another day make much difference?'

'I have to see someone. It's important.'

Leo got up at the sound of voices as Damien returned, Macey following closely behind.

'I think Kerri should see the medics,' Leo said.

'I need to rest a bit longer, that's all.'

65

Macey said nothing.

'Let me see that hand,' Leo said.

He took it in his very gently. Her thumb was twice the size it should be and the joint was swollen.

'Where's the nearest doctor?' Damien asked.

Macey frowned.

'I can't think what all the fuss is about. You heard what your sister said. She should know. It's her thumb.'

Kerri felt herself flush as Leo released her hand.

'Can I have a word, Leo?' Macey said suddenly.

'Of course. I've something in the Volvo I want you to glance at. Now could be a good time.'

Left alone, Kerri sighed.

'I'm such a nuisance. But my thumb is painful.'

'It is not your fault,' Damien said, looking unhappy.

Macey and Leo were back now.

'I'll drive you to the community hospital in Rawthwaite, Kerri,' Leo said with calm assurance. 'The accident and emergency unit there will advise you.'

Kerri made up her mind. At worst the hospital would tell her off for wasting their time but at least it would seem like permission to get going on her journey.

'Thanks, Leo,' she said quietly.

Macey sighed.

'Hurry up, then. We've got work to do.'

Kerri smiled at Damien encouragingly but she didn't look at Macey again. Her triumphant smile would be a little too much to bear.

'So.' Leo had reversed his car with expertise and they set off over the bridge. 'You're anxious to leave us, Kerri?'

'Things to do,' she said. 'And I expect you have, too.'

'Mine can wait. Your hand's really painful, isn't it?'

'A bit. The thumb mostly.'

'Then we're going to the right place.'

'I might be wasting their time.'

Damien laughed.

'I hope so, for your sake.'

Kerri leaned back in her seat and tried to appreciate the sun shining on the reservoir and the pair of swans swimming through it and leaving wakes of glittering water. But it was difficult because she was sitting so near Leo.

He found a space in the hospital car park. Then he jumped down to open the passenger door for her and to help her out too. Her arm flooded with warmth at his touch.

'Are you all right?'

She nodded as they walked to the main door. At the reception desk he explained what had happened and they were shown where to wait for the practice nurse.

'Practice nurse?' Leo muttered as they sat down. 'I don't think I like the sound of that. You'd think they'd go for someone already qualified.'

Kerri giggled.

Leo smiled.

'That's more like it.'

'You say you've got things to do,' she said. 'Why not do them while I am here?'

'You don't mind? I won't be long.'

'I could be a while.'

She moved to sit near the pile of magazines and picked one up, relieved that he'd taken up her suggestion. She had caused enough trouble already.

He was back by the time she emerged from the room she had been ushered into only a short while ago. He glanced at her bandaged hand.

'Good news?'

'Well, I'm not sure. I can't drive.'

'Is it still painful?'

'A bit. A lot, really. I've just taken some painkillers.'

'You need a hot drink,' he said. 'We'll get one here, then you can tell me about it. Or I know just the place, if you can hang on for about twenty minutes.'

He drove up the steep main street and out of the town, branching off soon afterwards, the road climbing higher.

68

'What did they say?'

'Nothing's broken. I've to give it at least a day and then go back for an X-ray if the swelling doesn't go down.'

'So you can't do anything at Alder Knowle.'

'I can't drive, either. It's agony to try to use my hand.'

'So how about forgetting our troubles for a while? I don't think either of us will be missed.'

She tried to smile and then looked with awe at huge boulders strewn on the rough hillside.

'What on earth are those doing there?'

'You haven't seen anything yet,' he said.

They reached a car park and from here Kerri gazed at jagged pinnacles of rock.

'Incredible!'

'This way, Kerri.'

She followed him up a narrow path to a rock formation that towered up like a giant stalagmite.

'Plenty more to see yet,' he said.

Awed she saw more magnificent rock formations ahead as they rounded a bend. There were people wandering among them, some attempting to climb some lower ones.

'They need ropes to do that. And proper equipment.'

'Do they come from your place to do rock climbing?'

'Yes. I've never tried to do any myself but I live in hope I'll be invited to join them one day.'

She shuddered.

'It's never appealed to me.' She thought of André in far-off Switzerland making the most of his last day in the Alps. She had never been able to understand the fascination of climbing. Lucy liked rock climbing, too. She gave a little sigh as she thought of her friend.

Leo looked at her enquiringly. 'Something wrong?'

'My friend Lucy would love it here. She'd be up that rock face over there as soon as look at it.'

He laughed.

'You have sensible friends.'

Now the path widened and led out to an open area of grass. Beyond was a large stone building on rising ground.

'There's a café in there through the shop,' Leo said. 'Lecture rooms and exhibition upstairs where you can discover how all this came about at the end of the last Ice Age. But I thought we'd get coffees from the kiosk over there and use a picnic table. What d'you think?'

'Perfect,' she said.

'Find a seat then, Kerri.'

She did so, choosing one that gave the best view over the rocks to the countryside beyond that stretched into the mauve distance. Even though she was looking down on them the huge boulders still looked impressive. She

70

watched a party of school children with their teachers wandering about, most of them sketching what they saw and letting out squeals of awe every now and again.

She pulled out her phone and checked there was a good signal before clicking on the number for Roseleaf. She needed to notify the staff that she couldn't get back as planned and this was a good place to do it.

Her call was picked up at once as if Carol, sitting there in the office at André's desk, twiddling strands of long blonde hair, was expecting the call.

'Roseleaf Nurseries. How can I help you?'

'Carol, it's Kerri.'

'Kerri? Oh, hi!' Her voice sounded uncertain.

'Is everything all right?'

'I don't know. André just phoned.'

'He did?'

'He's not coming back. Not yet, anyway. He's decided to stay on for a bit. Another couple of days at least.'

This was disturbing news.

'But why?'

'I don't know, Kerri. He's not been in touch with you?'

Kerri shook her head and then realised Carol couldn't see her down there in Bristol.

'No. I'd better ring off in case he's trying to get through to me,' she said. 'You can manage without me for a day or two more, can't you,

71

Carol? I'll get back to you.'

Kerri put her phone down on the table and stared at it. Should she ring André or wait for his call? His decision to stay longer away from Roseleaf was so unlike André it was bizarre. There could be a very good reason, of course, but she wished she knew what it was.

## The Silver Jugs

Leo walked back to the table, carrying the two mugs of coffee with care. He pushed a mug across to Kerri, relieved he'd managed to get both here without spilling any.

'Here you are then, Kerri.'

She looked up, startled.

'What's up?' he said as he slid into the seat opposite.

'I'm expecting a call.'

'An important one?'

'I think so.'

'Well, drink up, Kerri. It'll do you good. Things can't be as bad as all that.'

She looked as if she thought they were. She cleared her throat, raised her mug to her lips and then put it down again.

The vulnerable expression in her eyes hurt him. He wanted to comfort her but didn't know how.

'I picked up this leaflet for you,' he said

72

fishing it out of his pocket and handing it to her.

The colourful scene on the front showed the place looking really attractive with soaring rocks outlined against a vivid sky. The information inside about the formation at the end of the last Ice Age was interesting but she merely glanced at it before putting it down. Her phone rang. She jumped and fumbled for her phone.

'D'you want me to leave you in peace?' he asked.

She motioned that it was all right to stay where he was.

'Hi, Damien,' she said into the phone. 'Yes, I'm OK. We're almost on the way back. They took my injury seriously at the hospital. I shan't be able to drive.'

She listened to him for a moment.

'Yes, it does matter. André will be home soon. I must be there.'

Another silence as her brother, on the other end, was obviously trying to persuade her to make the best of things. Kerri laid down the phone to click it off.

'I've got to stay on at Alder Knowle,' she said to Leo, sounding hopeless.

'That's no problem is it? I thought that was the idea. I know Macey wants you to stay longer.'

'She wants Damien to stay.' Kerri hesitated for a moment. 'I could book in somewhere in

73

Rawthwaite. The hospital said to go back if the swelling doesn't go down.'

'What would you do with yourself all day?'

She shrugged.

'Much better to stay at Alder Knowle,' he said. 'You'll have left your belongings there, I take it?'

'Oh. I'd forgotten that.'

Leo frowned. He hated to see her so defeated and all because of this André she seemed upset at not seeing. He took a sip of his coffee, put down his mug and stared at it.

'I must stop feeling so sorry for myself,' she said, trying to smile. 'Of course it's best for me to be back at Alder Knowle for the night. And who says the swelling won't go down anyway?'

'That's the spirit. Never give in.'

'I don't usually,' she said, her voice humble.

'But this time it's different?'

She was silent.

'Fancy a look at the exhibition?'

She shook her head.

'Then let's go, shall we? I'll take the mugs back.'

They walked back to the car in silence. On the drive back to Alder Knowle neither said very much. She interested Leo because he had never met any girl quite like her before.

This André was a lucky chap.

Macey was nowhere to be seen when they arrived. Leo parked his vehicle and went in search of her as Damien appeared in the

74

kitchen doorway.

'André's staying longer in Switzerland' she said.

'You've heard from him?'

She shook her head.

'I phoned Roseleaf.'

'And?'

'And nothing. Carol said he didn't say why.'

'Have you tried to get in touch with him since?'

'I thought he might be trying to get through to me, and then it was too late and there was no signal.'

'How's your thumb now?'

She glanced at it.

'It feels huge.'

'I'll get your bag and show you where we're staying.'

The building nearby that had been converted into a holiday cottage was roomier than it looked from outside. Maybe it was because it was sparsely furnished, Kerri thought, eyeing the folded camp beds leaning against one of the two chairs in the sitting-room. There was an empty bookcase against one of the walls but that was all.

'There are two bedrooms upstairs,' Damien said as he came in with her luggage. 'I've dumped my stuff in the one at the back. So you just relax, Kerri.'

She found that hard to do because her thumb was beginning to throb. She had far too much to think about anyway with the bombshell from Carol. Later she would phone André from the hill where she could get a signal.

She wandered through to the kitchen and saw that there was a breakfast bar with a couple of stools that slid underneath. She could hear Damien's footsteps as he came clattering down the stairs.

'It's odd. Macey's only left one lot of bedding. I'd better get the rest now. Will you be OK here for a bit?'

'Of course. I'll take a look upstairs.'

The room allocated to her had a far-reaching view across the reservoir to the distant hills. She rested her right hand on the window-sill and leaned on it. Down below, Macey appeared from the direction of the house as a grey car drove over the bridge and pulled up by the wall. A man got out in a pink jacket. The estate agent!

Kerri watched, fascinated, to see what would happen. To her surprise, Macey appeared to be smiling as he produced a clipboard from his briefcase. Had Macey decided to put the property on the market after all? They talked some more and then he followed her indoors.

Kerri went downstairs. She heard voices and the door was pushed open. Macey looked surprised to see her.

'Kerri?'

76

'Damien's looking for you,' Kerri said.

'So you've come back? I might have known you'd find a way to stay. But it doesn't do to be too possessive.'

Kerri looked at her in astonishment.

'Hit your thumb against your car door deliberately, I suppose, to get Leo's sympathy?' Macey turned to her companion.

'Feel free to look round. A holiday let, as I said. Bound to get booked up all through the year in this area.'

He smiled at Kerri.

'Charles Brownley. We've met, briefly.'

'Hello again.'

He peered round the room with narrowed eyes.

'You expect your clients to bring their own furniture?'

Macey looked annoyed.

'I haven't kitted the place out yet, obviously.'

'So you've had no bookings to date?'

'I told you. I'm not ready for that. But this is a money-spinner for whoever buys the property.'

'There's no proof of that without bookings to show for the coming season,' he said. 'Most prospective purchasers will assume the place is too isolated.'

'You can't know that.'

'You want a quick sale? I suggest you consider selling this cottage as a separate entity. I have someone in mind who would pay a good price for somewhere like this.'

'The cottage goes with the house, or not at all,' said Macey firmly. 'That's the way I want it.'

'On its own the house will do better as well.'

'You sound very sure.'

'I'm the expert.' He gazed at her levelly.

Macey left, slamming the door shut behind her,

Kerri made a movement to go, too. This was Macey's business, not hers, and she needed to contact André.

She climbed only halfway up the hill this time. But for some reason she was reluctant to dial André's number and stood for a moment looking at the phone in her hand.

André hadn't tried to contact her, assuming, she supposed, that she was back working at Roseleaf and his message would be passed to her. She sent a text to say where she was, and why, and asked about him. Then she found a handy outcrop of limestone and sat down against it to give him the chance to reply if he were free to do so.

She looked down at the house and the cottage nearby, wondering if Charles Brownley had completed his inspection. Maybe she shouldn't have left him alone there because their belongings were in the cottage. She smiled at her suspicious thoughts, remembering that he had given her his card and Macey must surely trust him.

Now was the chance to send Lucy a quick text to tell her about her change of plan and the reason for it. This was quickly done and after another few minutes Kerri struggled to her feet since there had been no reply to her text to André as yet. She would try him again later and then contact Carol again to see if she had any more news.

She set off. There might be something odd going on at the cottage and she'd feel happier when she had checked.

She found Damien in the hall of the house stacking boxes in the corner by the front door.

'Unwanted items,' he said when he saw Kerri. 'Not a lot of value but they could be useful to someone. I suggested we do a car boot sale.'

'The bedding?' Kerri reminded him.

'Oh, that. Macey'll see to it.'

'But not just yet, of course.'

He looked at her in surprise.

'Are you OK, Kerri?'

She was aware of the bitter tone in her voice and attempted to lighten it.

'Macey doesn't like me. You haven't picked up on that?'

Damien made an exclamation of disbelief.

'She's accused me of injuring my thumb deliberately.'

'Surely not.'

'She thinks it's a ruse on my part.'

'To stay longer? But surely it's already decided that I'll stay to help her as long as I'm needed?'

'You've got it wrong, Damien. She wants me to head off and leave you here so you and she will have a clear run.'

'Oh, come on, Kerri, You're imagining things. I don't know why you've got it in for poor Macey.'

'Because she's got it in for me.'

'I can't believe that.'

'Or won't,' Kerri muttered, turning away.

By mid-afternoon Kerri could bear her inaction no longer. All day Damien and Macey had been involved upstairs and only emerging from their task for a late lunch. The look of weariness on Damien's face was disturbing.

Kerri came to a decision. She would write André a long letter explaining how she felt and saying that she believed they had come to the end of the road as far as their engagement was concerned and she wanted to be free.

On a separate sheet she would write her letter of resignation from Roseleaf, because Carol would need that for the records. But before that she would try to contact André again by phone. Writing the letter would be a difficult job, needing plenty of deliberation.

She sat at the breakfast bar in the kitchen to write, pausing often. When she had finished she read it through, dissatisfied but unable to do any better for the moment. At least the letter was written and she felt better for that.

Near the shed at the top of the garden might get her the mobile signal she wanted. She headed for the gate in the wall. She found that she got enough signal but the results were the same. No message of any sort from André. Worried she rang Carol at Roseleaf to check if she'd heard anything more but there was no reply.

If she'd heard nothing by tomorrow, she would try to contact his hotel. And then she would post her letter.

She glanced at her watch. Maybe she should check on how the others were doing at the house and see if they needed her help with anything, one-handed as she was.

In the sitting-room Macey and Damien, their heads close together, were examining some silver objects.

Damien looked up as he heard her.

'Look at these, Kerri. A set of five jugs, all made at the same time. There's an assay mark on them all, so that dates them, and they're in excellent condition.'

'Are they valuable?' Macey lifted one up.

Damien ran his fingers over the largest one.

'Look, Kerri, there's a family design in the engraving, wouldn't you say? The same on all of them.'

Kerri picked up one but Macey snatched it from her. Damien's look of surprise would have amused Kerri if she hadn't been so annoyed. She picked up another instead.

'My brother wants me to take a look for myself.' She thought this might trigger a retort to alert Damien to Macey's enmity towards her but this time Macey managed to control herself.

Kerri examined the pretty little jug she was holding and ran her fingers over the engraved initials entwined with what looked like heather and waving grasses.

'I haven't seen anything like this before,' she said.

'It's certainly unique.'

Kerri knew that Damien wasn't prepared to estimate the value of the pieces but she could feel his excitement.

'I think these should be sent to auction, Macey.'

The dimple in her cheek deepening as she smiled.

'Would you like one for yourself, Damien?'

He looked shocked.

'And break up the set?'

'Why not? You deserve it. I'll have four of them left.'

He smiled.

'The five jugs together are a wonderful collection, Macey, and worth so much more as a complete set. It would be a foolish thing to separate them.'

'Damien's not hinting you should give him the lot,' Kerri said, smiling too.

'I know that!' Macey looked at Kerri with dislike.

'Sorry. I was joking.'

'A fine joke!'

Damien looked startled at the venom in Macey's voice.

'Just a minute, Macey . . .' he began.

Macey leaped up.

'I'm going for a shower. We've done enough here for the moment. I have an account at the Old Oak in Alderfield, Damien. Book yourselves a table for two. I shall make my own arrangements.'

'Well, that's that, then.' Damien was still holding the smallest jug in the set. He stared down at it for a moment and then reached for the creamy-grey tissue paper at his side and began to wrap each jug in turn.

'These are lovely things and should fetch a fair price at auction,' he said, as if nothing untoward had happened.

'Which is more than Macey deserves.'

'Don't be hard on her, Kerri. It's not like you. She's had a hard time of it. She needs someone to look out for her.'

With a huge effort of will Kerri said nothing. Her thumb was still throbbing and the swelling hadn't begun to go down yet, which was worrying.

She wished she were anywhere but here, a prisoner in the home of someone she had distrusted from their first meeting. Macey was acting so strangely it was almost frightening. They didn't belong here, she and Damien.

'So are you going to phone the Old Oak?'

Damien shrugged as he got to his feet.

'Have we enough money? I don't want Macey to pay.'

'I wish we had some food at the cottage.'

'You could have got some in Rawthwaite.'

'Easy for you to say. I had other things to think about.'

They glared at each other.

This was getting them nowhere, Kerri thought. What had happened to them that were at each other's throats like this? Macey, of course, although Damien couldn't see it.

'We're stuck if you won't let me drive,' Damien said.

'We could walk.'

'And come back in the dark without a torch?'

'I'm going back to the cottage,' Kerri said, near to tears.

'Wait, Kerri. We'll walk if you like.'

He smiled at her and she smiled back. They didn't often fall out but when they did she felt so alone it hurt.

His eyes brightened.

'I've got an idea.'

Kerri followed him down the stairs and saw he had fished out the telephone directory from beneath the table.

'We'll get a taxi,' he said kneeling down to

open it.

Seconds later he looked up, smiling, his finger keeping the place he had found.

'A Rawthwaite firm. What time shall I say?'

Kerri glanced at her watch. She hadn't brought many clothes with her but she needed time to change.

'Half six?'

It was soon done and the reservation made at the Old Oak.

'Clever or what?' Damien said smiling.

'You surprise me.'

Damien stretched.

'You're right. We can't sponge off Macey all the time.'

With the prospect of a pleasant leisurely meal alone with Damien ahead of her Kerri could afford to be magnanimous.

'We have to be fair to her. She said she had other plans and we have to respect that.'

Finding a pile of bedding in her room was a pleasant surprise. It would have to wait until later because changing into her blue shirt and clean jeans would take longer than usual because of her bloated and painful thumb.

At last she was ready.

They waited for the taxi in front of the house. Kerri buttoned her jacket against the breeze, shivering a little.

'I don't like the look of those clouds,' Damien said.

The distant hills looked gloomy now and

85

the water in the reservoir was like dirty glass. Thank goodness for the taxi.

It came moments later.

As they drove Kerri wondered if Macey's plans included Leo and then resolved to banish them from her mind for this evening at least and enjoy herself. The Old Oak was a small, friendly place with tables and chairs scattered invitingly on the grass outside overlooking the Alder. The front of the building was ivy-clad and the door stood open.

Inside the rough tables looked as if they had been here since the place was built. Kerri expected to be served by someone elderly in a long dress and shawl. Instead, the girl who appeared looked only a few years older than herself.

'Hi, I'm Annie.' She ran her hands down the side of her jeans. 'Are you wanting a meal?' Her voice was warm with just a hint of Yorkshire accent in it.

'Hi, Annie,' Damien said. 'I'm Damien and this is Kerri.'

She nodded and smiled at Kerri.

'Are you here on holiday? It's a grand place.'

'Not exactly.'

'We were surprised when you booked the table in the name of Treghennel.'

'But that's our name.'

'That may be, but we thought it would be Macey coming to make another scene.'

There was a second's silence.

'She wouldn't have booked a table if she intended to do that, would she?'

'You know her?'

Kerri nodded.

'She recommended we come here.'

Annie laughed.

'She's a one. Wait till I tell Max.'

What had Macey done to earn Annie's condemnation?

Then Annie's tone seemed to change to professional.

'So, sir, what can I get for you?'

'Sir, now, is it?'

'Just doing my job.' Annie's voice sounded prim but her eyes were dancing.

They chose shepherd's pie and while they waited for it Damien looked thoughtfully around at the empty tables. Kerri wondered if he was wishing Lucy was with them. Annie returned with cutlery, glasses and a jug of water. 'Thanks. That'll be fine in the way of drinks, won't it, Kerri? We'll have coffee afterwards.'

Kerri clumsily picked up her fork with her left hand.

'I don't know how thumbless people manage.'

'That looks bad.' Annie frowned. 'How did you do it?'

'Knocked it when a car nearly drove ours into the ditch.'

'When was this?'

'This morning. I've got to go back to the hospital if the swelling doesn't go down.'

'Annie!' came a shout from the kitchen.

She sprang to attention.

'Coming, Max.'

Back again with their order she seemed inclined to linger but then thought better of it.

'Give a call if you need anything,' she said.

'This looks good.' Damien poured water from the jug.

Afterwards, Annie was back to recite a list of desserts.

'Not for me,' Kerri said. 'But I'm sure my brother will.'

'Your brother!' Annie smiled. 'I can see a likeness.'

'Most people can't, even though we're twins.'

'I'm not a bit like my brother, either. But he's four years older than me, and much cleverer. Except when it comes to Macey Treghennel. He's only just met her because he's been in Canada until recently. I don't know what he sees in her.' A light seemed to dawn in her eyes. 'You must be the girl he met down at Alder Knowle!'

'Your brother met me?'

'When he was down taking a look at the cottage.'

'The estate agent, Charles Brownley, is your brother?'

Annie nodded.

'That cottage would be so right for Mum and Dad.'

'Annie!'

'Apple pie and custard,' Damien said quickly.

She was off at once and then returned looking crestfallen.

Kerri leaned back in her seat. Damien wiped his mouth as he finished.

'That was good. I couldn't manage any more.'

'There's coffee yet,' she reminded him.

When it came Kerri looked at the large pot.

'How about bringing another cup and joining us?'

Annie flitted away and returned with a cup and saucer.

'We're not busy tonight. I can take time off. We've a crowd in tomorrow for the Thursday quiz so they're saving themselves for that. It's always quiet on a Wednesday.'

Kerri poured the coffee and handed hers to Annie. There was no hurry for them to return to Alder Knowle and it was pleasant here. As she listened to Annie telling them of everything that went on in the district a warm feeling crept round her heart. She and Damien seemed to have found a friend, and it felt good.

'Have you lived round here all your life, Annie?' Damien asked.

'Mostly. I'm between jobs at the moment and glad to work here for Max and live at home.'

'So what's your line?'

'I did secretarial work for various firms about the place for a while. But after a bit Mum became ill and I wanted to be near home to help out. She's fine again now but that's why they want to downsize now, you see.'

'So your brother is on the look-out for somewhere suitable for them?'

'He'll move into their house permanently when he does and I'll move out. We've never got on.'

'You'll be homeless!'

'Jobless, too, if I've nowhere to live.'

She didn't look too upset at the prospect, Kerri thought, so perhaps there was something in the pipeline.

'But won't it be too quiet for your parents at Alder Knowle?' Damien asked.

Kerri smiled.

'There's birdwatching.'

'Got it in one! Dad'll be in his element, right on the spot. He takes after his daughter.' She laughed. 'That's me. I started up the local Ornithology Club, you see. And Mum'll get a bit of peace for her painting.'

Damien looked interested.

'She's a painter?'

'She's planning on starting a group of people who like to paint outdoors. Lots of space for that round Alder Knowle.'

'And good views to paint,' Kerri agreed.

'So what's the cottage like then? Any good?'

'It's where we're staying tonight. Large sitting-room and kitchen, two bedrooms and bathroom upstairs.'

'And some garden at one side,' Kerri added.

'I wish I could see it.'

Damien glanced at his watch.

'We'll have to get going soon. I'll ring for a taxi.'

'No need. I'll finish early tonight and I'll drive you. I want a quick look at the property and you need a lift back.'

'But it's dark,' Kerri said.

'It's the inside I want to check. Charles wouldn't tell me anything about it. He gets suspicious of my motives. He'll think I'll accuse him of saying any hovel will do just to get our parents out of the house so he can take over.'

'But surely they'd have some say in it?'

'He's very persuasive. He can get anyone to agree to anything if he puts his mind to it. And Dad wants to be near the reservoir, so I know Charles'll play on that.'

'The cottage is really good,' Kerri said.

'I'd like to see it for myself. And you won't need a taxi.'

Damien smiled at her.

'Could it be that Charles takes after his sister?'

Annie laughed.

'Could be. So how about it?'

Put like that it sounded simple. Damien drained the last of his coffee and stood up.

'It doesn't sound as if we'll get rid of you in a hurry, Annie, so we'll give in. But I need to pay the bill first.'

He strode to the bar.

Annie winked at Kerri.

'You know what brothers are and Charles is the worst of the lot. If your hand's still swollen in the morning I'll drive you down to Rawthwaite. That's a deal.'

The bill was soon settled and they went outside into the rainy dark. A spotlight illuminated the front courtyard where Annie's car lurked in the shadow by the fence. She opened the passenger seat for Kerri while Damien climbed into the back.

Before Kerri could get in too her mobile rang. She fished it out of her pocket. Lucy!

Turning her back and hoping that Damien couldn't hear what she as saying she clicked to be able to hear her.

'At last, Kerri,' came Lucy's clear voice. 'So glad I've caught you. How are things?'

'Looking up a bit,' Kerri said cautiously. 'Just had a lovely meal. I'm hoping to get the all clear to drive soon.'

'Do you want me to come and get you?'

It was a generous offer and tears sprang to Kerri's eyes.

'I may take you up on that,' she said. 'You're a good friend, Lucy. I can't say any more now.'

Kerri clicked off her phone. She rubbed her hand across her eyes as she got in the car and they set off.

Annie drove slowly with her tongue protruding between her lips. Kerri could feel Damien's tension behind her by the way he breathed deeply every now and again.

'A tricky bit of road this, especially in the rain. I passed my test a couple of weeks ago. It makes such a difference to my life.'

And to other road users, too, Kerri thought as Annie swerved for no reason at all.

They drove along the track to Alder Knowle at not much more than walking pace. At last they reached the bridge.

'I'd better park out of sight,' Annie said.

'On the other side of the track?' Damien said helpfully. 'There's bit of a lay-by along here.'

'I know it well,' Annie said. 'The bird hide down there is my main passion, you see. Dad's, too, which is good. That's why this cottage could be perfect for them.'

With a lot of grinding as she inched backwards and forwards, the car was facing the way Annie wanted it. They jerked to a stop, she switched off everything and they got out.

'There's a torch somewhere,' she said.

Then they heard the approach of another

car.

'I'll not stop after all,' she said quickly. 'I know the sound of that engine. Pretend I'm a taxi. I'll come back tomorrow to take a look, shall I?'

The next moment she was back in her car and the lights switched on. Damien pulled Kerri back against the wall as the engine sprang to life.

'She's lethal,' he muttered as Annie drove off.

'But very kind.'

The other car slowed down and drove into the yard. Kerri and Damien stayed where they were, not knowing if the returning Macey would want them to make their presence known at this moment although she must have guessed they were there.

It seemed not. They heard the sound of muted voices and the front door of the house opening and closing. Kerri looked towards it, surprised that Macey was content to ignore them when previously she had delighted in letting them know about her planned evening out with Leo.

'That's that, then,' Damien said. He gave a huge yawn. 'Quite a day, one way or another. I'm ready for bed.'

'Me, too.'

The trouble was, she still had to make up hers and even with the duvet it was difficult with the use of only one hand.

Damien, too exhausted to be able to think straight, had gone immediately upstairs, refusing the offer of coffee.

Kerri made some for herself and sat at the breakfast bar to drink it. She thought of her unposted letter and wished it was already on its way. But tomorrow it would be, and the walk to Alderfield would present no problems in daylight. And Macey would be delighted to have her out of the way.

## Call From André

Kerri was right about that. Macey's expression softened as soon as she mentioned it at breakfast next day.

But Damien looked doubtful.

'How will you get back?'

'It's beautiful weather,' Kerri said. 'I'll enjoy the walk.'

'I'll come with you.'

'I'm not likely to meet dangerous attackers in daylight.'

Macey hesitated in the act of pouring Damien's tea and let some of the liquid spill on to the table. She dabbed at it angrily with the tea cloth.

'I need you here, Damien,' she said. 'We're late getting started and there's a lot to do. It's nine o'clock already.'

He seemed to remember suddenly that Annie had promised a visit.

'Oh, Kerri, you might meet Annie on the way.'

'Annie Brownley?' Macey sounded annoyed.

'We met her at the Old Oak last night.'

'You did, did you?' Macey pursed her lips. 'I've been making enquiries. I've been told that there's just time to have my items accepted for the next auction, if I'm quick about it. You must stay here, Damien, so I can call you if I need you to give an accurate description if they need it.'

He nodded.

'Do we know when the auction is?'

'Soon.'

Carefully Kerri put down her knife. Couldn't Damien see that Macey was being awkward on purpose?

'I'll be off as soon as we've finished.'

'But not until the clearing up is done,' Macey snapped.

Damien smiled.

'We'll both do it.'

Fair enough, Kerri thought. Between the two of them it wouldn't take long even with only three hands. She felt sure that Annie would turn up, but it wouldn't do for Macey to see her assessing the cottage. Kerri would set off on foot soon and meet her along the track.

Immediately the meal was finished Macey

went off to the hall to use the telephone. Kerri cleared the table, a slow job with only one useful hand and piled the things on the draining board while Damien ran hot water in the sink.

'We could leave the things to drain,' he said.

'And have Macey accuse me of falling down on the job?'

Damien laughed.

'So how will you manage?'

Kerri grabbed hold of the tea towel, placed it flat on the work top and put a washed plate on top of it. Then with her good hand it was possible to get it dry.

'It'll take you a long time,' he said.

'There's another cloth. You can help me dry.'

For answer he flicked water at her and she laughed. This was more like the old Damien.

By the time Macey returned looking flushed and triumphant everything was done. Kerri returned to the cottage across the wet yard to collect her shoulder bag and check her phone was in it.

This morning the water in the reservoir sparkled in the sunshine again and the hills on the other side looked faintly golden with the changing season.

Down in St Ives it would still feel like summer, she thought, with late tourists enjoying the golden sand and blue sky. She thought of the antique shop and wondered if

Damien thought of the business he might be losing. It seemed unlikely, with his interest in Macey growing by the day.

She had gone some way along the track before she saw Annie's vehicle and was standing well back as it drew up alongside her, avoiding a puddle. The door rattled open and Annie got out.

'This is unexpected,' she said. 'Trying to escape or something?'

'Something like that. I've got a letter to post.'

'Don't tell me—our Macey's on the warpath?'

She opened the door on Kerri's side.

'Jump in and I'll turn just here,' she said. 'I'd better not be seen by Madam and ordered off the premises.'

Kerri smiled as she did as she was told.

'So,' Annie said as she got her car pointing in the right direction. 'We're heading off, are we? I'm game for that.'

'I'm so glad you came, Annie,' Kerri said. 'I needed to get away for a bit.'

'Rawthwaite it is, then.' Annie had a smile in her voice. 'You can tell me all about it as we go.'

Kerri leaned back in her seat and tried not to flinch every time it seemed that the car might swerve off the road.

'It's complicated,' Kerri said, wincing as a dog looked as if it was about to shoot across the road outside the Old Oak but changed its mind. The owner glared at the car as they passed. 'I'll fill you in with the rest when we park the car.'

In the event there was no opportunity because Annie got into a violent argument with another driver who thought that the parking place she had chosen to use should have been his.

'Come on, Kerri, let's get away from here,' Annie, said clutching her arm and dragging her towards the entrance. 'I like to use this car park at the top of the hill. The cheek of the man!'

'I think he was there first,' Kerri commented.

Annie, ignoring her, darted across the road.

'The war memorial's a good place to talk,' she said when Kerri joined her. 'It's about halfway down and there are seats. Lucky the rain stopped early.'

*     *     *

Leo clicked off his mobile and sat for a moment in his car overlooking the River Alder as it flowed sedately beneath the arches of the bridge at the bottom end of town. This morning Rawthwaite was bathed in a damp glow as the sun shone through a wisp of cloud that he hoped was the last of the rain clouds. There had been heavy rain here during the night from the look of the puddles in the car park and he was glad he had postponed his arrival to coincide with one of the clear periods forecasters had promised.

Macey had been very short with him when he phoned to ask after Kerri. But not for a moment did he believe that Kerri had overreacted as Macey implied. Her swollen thumb must genuinely worry her.

Leo got out of his car and stretched. No harm in wandering up to the hospital, he thought. He presumed her brother had brought her in and that's why Macey had sounded so exasperated. He was halfway up the main street when he saw Kerri on a seat by the war memorial. At first he didn't recognise who she was with.

Kerri looked up and saw him.

'Leo!' Her smile lit up her face and her eyes shone.

He felt a warm glow that she was pleased to see him.

'Macey seemed to think you were at the hospital.'

'Macey doesn't know everything.' The girl at Kerri's side, Annie Brownley, looked pleased.

He hesitated. There was something going on here.

'What did they say at Outpatients?'

Annie shrugged his question off.

'She has to go back and have it checked tomorrow, Friday, not today.'

'So what are you two doing here?'

'We'll need to swear you to secrecy!'

Kerri smiled.

'Take no notice of her, Leo. She drove me down to Rawthwaite so I can use the post office and then withdraw some cash from the bank.'

'We'd better get a move on,' Annie said. 'I've got to be back at Alderfield at twelve or Max will be livid.' She jumped up and pulled Kerri up with her.

'Mind if I walk down with you?' Leo said. 'And when you've done what you need to do how about joining me at the Riverside Café for some of their special ices?'

The grounds on either side of the river near where Leo had parked his car were extensive. They walked past the bandstand to the red-tiled building that was the Riverside Café where the tables and chairs outside had been freshly wiped dry and now gleamed in the sunshine.

'This is great,' Annie said when they had made their selection and were waiting for the ices to be brought out to them. 'But we can't stay long.'

'I can give Kerri a lift back,' Leo said with authority.

'Wait,' Kerri protested. 'I'm here, too, you know.'

'Sorry. Your friend has such a powerful presence.'

Annie grinned.

'That's what Max says. He says I overpower customers and he doesn't want me fraternising with them.'

'You did a good job with us last evening,' Kerri said. 'We liked it. We were feeling a bit out of things, Damien and I.'

Leo looked surprised.

'You were at the Old Oak? What happened to Macey?'

'You may well ask,' Annie said darkly. 'With my brother at that new place over Grassington way, if you please.'

Leo looked interested.

'She was?'

Their ices arrived, piled high in a profusion of nuts and glacé cherries. Annie fell on hers at once but Kerri ate hers slowly, savouring every mouthful.

Her phone call to André had been no more successful than before but she knew by contacting Roseleaf that he was expected back by Monday at the latest and with sudden resolution she had posted her letter.

Her feeling of relief was unbelievable. Sitting here in the sunshine in the company of two people she was fast regarding as friends was pleasant.

Annie put down her spoon and wiped her mouth with a tissue.

'Thanks, that was great. I'll have to go. See you around.'

Leo watched her walk jauntily across the grass and then turned to Kerri. There was a tenderness in his eyes as he looked at her and for a moment she felt uncomfortable. With André it had taken months to feel so attracted to him.

He cleared his throat.

'So, Kerri, how are you really? How is your hand?'

She didn't want to show him, because even with the bandage on he would see that swelling at the ball of the thumb was turning a yellowish colour and looked horrible.

'It looks painful. I think it should be seen to.'

'Tomorrow, Friday, they said.'

'No buts. It can't hurt to show up at the hospital.'

She hesitated.

'I can't take you back to Alder Knowle knowing you're in such pain. Don't deny it, Kerri.'

She felt warm in his concern and was glad to leave the decision to him. She nodded.

'And when we've got it seen to we'll come back here again,' he said. 'They do good bacon butties, I can vouch for that.'

'Sounds great.'

'Come on, then, what are we waiting for?'

They walked to the hospital because it wasn't far and the parking there was almost non-existent. Leo talked of his latest seed test that seemed to prove that a particular type of carrot seed was far away the best for the conditions at Alderbeck. She suspected that he was trying to distract her and was grateful.

By the time Kerri had been seen and her thumb attended to the clock on the church tower was striking half past twelve. Her hand was bandaged again now and her thumb felt a lot easier now that an injection had dulled the pain. She was told to return the next day to have her dressing renewed.

They paused by the kerb to wait for a van trundling up the steep street to pass and Kerri felt suddenly dizzy. At once Leo's arm was around her.

'Lean on me for a moment, Kerri.'

'I'm sorry,' she said. 'I'll be all right.'

'I shouldn't have let you walk.'

She took a deep breath as the dizziness began to clear but he didn't move his arm until he was quite sure she felt better.

'Can you manage to walk the rest of the way now?' he asked.

'Perfectly,' she said and took a step to prove it.

'You never give in, do you, Kerri?' he said.

She flushed at his admiring tone.

'I don't really think about it.'

As they walked slowly for the rest of the way to the riverbank, Kerri was conscious of Leo's presence in a way she hadn't been before. Maybe it was the freedom she felt after posting her letter to André even if he hadn't received it yet. Or perhaps the softness in the air compared with the breeziness at Alder Knowle had something to do with it.

Leo led her to a table a little way from the others in the shade of a willow tree that was starting to shed its leaves.

'I'll get us a hot drink first,' he said. 'Then we'll decide what to do.'

She thought they had already decided. Or perhaps he was regretting his suggestion when it came to the point. He probably had things to do back at his testing shed and hadn't realised how late it was getting.

He was soon back with two mugs of steaming tea.

'This was the quickest,' he said as he sat down and passed one across to her.

'You're in a hurry now?'

'Only to get you a hot drink in case you pass out.'

She rested her bandaged hand on the table.

'Thanks, Leo. I'll do the same for you one day.'

He laughed.

'I hope I never look as white-faced as you do.'

Quickly she rubbed her cheek.

'This tea will work wonders.' She took a sip from her cup.

'I can see it's doing the trick already,' he said. 'Your colour's coming back by the second.'

She felt that it must be because she felt so much better. 'I suppose it was the shock back there,' she said.

'So, what's it going to be? Shall I get a menu?'

She hesitated, thinking of Damien and Macey perhaps noticing that it was now lunchtime and she hadn't shown up.

'What's wrong?'

'Nothing really,' she said. 'The others might wonder where I am, though.'

'No problem,' he said pulling out his mobile. 'Ah, the answer phone. I'll leave a message.'

She let out a breath of relief.

'I was afraid it would be Macey.'

'You're not afraid of her, surely? She's a great girl.'

She smiled.

'If you say so.'

She wasn't afraid exactly, she thought, just slightly concerned at Macey's likely reaction when she knew she was with Leo.

'Anyway, all's well,' he said. 'So, now, what's it to be?'

She smiled.

'Bacon butties sound just fine.'

Never had they tasted so good oozing with bacon fat that sank into the soft baps. Leo bought them each another and then some coffee. As they sat drinking it a few more leaves floated down from the willow tree and joined others on the ground. The trees on the other side of the river had a russet glow to them that looked beautiful against the blue sky.

*     *     *

It was mid-afternoon by the time Leo drew up in the yard near the cottage. There was no one about and the place had a feeling of desertion as if it had been abandoned for hours.

'I don't like to leave you here on your own,' he said.

Kerri laughed.

'It's not the dead of night in the depths of winter.'

He took her hands in his.

'I don't want to leave you at all,' he said, his voice husky, 'but I've things I have to do back at Alderbeck.'

'More testing?' she said.

They hadn't talked of their gardening interests during the meal, so there had been no disagreements about laying out the perfect garden to disturb the pleasant interlude.

'It could be a likely breakthrough,' he said. 'And it has to be checked within the next hour.'

She didn't ask what it was. His obvious enthusiasm was enough to indicate how important this was to him.

'It's been great, Kerri, in spite of the

107

emergency,' he said. 'I'll be in touch about a lift down tomorrow.'

'Thanks, Leo. I appreciate it.'

His mind seemed to be on other things as he bent and kissed her cheek.

'Look after yourself.'

When he had gone she didn't go into the cottage but wandered across the yard and into the walled garden that she was beginning to think of as her own. She felt the pressure of Leo's lips still and wanted to saviour the moment in a place she loved to be.

The clouds of earlier in the day had drifted away and a slight breeze ruffled her hair as she climbed slowly to the top of the garden. Leo had mended the latch on the shed door and it opened easily for her to reach inside for one of the garden chairs.

It was still warm enough to linger here for a while thinking of how she would tackle clearing the area if it were really her own. It would be easy enough to have a bonfire further down in the centre of the plot and get rid of most of the dry stuff.

She thought of the smell of smoke on autumn evenings. Maybe Leo's idea of a digger to come and clear the rest was a good one after all and they could start afresh.

They? She pulled herself up short. She was presuming a lot here and must stop it at once before she began to believe in her own fantasy.

At last she got up to go, folded the garden

chair and put it back in the shed.

Her phone rang. Startled, she pulled it out. She saw, with a thumping of her heart, a familiar number on the screen.

'Hello,' she said. 'André, is that really you?'

It was, but he sounded different, awkward and slightly stilted as if what he had to say was going to be difficult and he didn't know the best way to start.

'Kerri, we need to talk.'

She was silent. Of course they needed to talk, but this sounded odd when she had been the one trying to contact him. Hearing his voice so unexpectedly was upsetting in a way she hadn't expected.

'Are you still there, Kerri?'

Her mouth felt dry.

'What is it, André? Are you all right? I've been trying to get hold of you. Carol told me you were staying on. Where are you now?'

He hesitated, and in that brief beat of time she knew everything that mattered without being told. The cold feeling deep inside her strengthened until she felt turned to ice.

'It's complicated, Kerri,' he said. 'I have to tell you . . . I'm bringing someone home with me.'

'André, what do you mean?'

'She's the cousin of this chap I met. She wants to see England and I said she could come with me if she liked. So we're coming on Monday. It was the first flight she could get

109

and I was able to change mine.'

'You're still in Switzerland?'

'We'll be back in a few days.'

'You mean . . .' She fought a desire to dissolve into tears. In the light of the letter she had posted to him today, what right had she to feel so distressed?

'I'm sorry,' he said.

She took a deep breath. He was trying to tell her that they were finished and she couldn't quite take it in.

'You need to tell me more, André,' she said.

'I will, Kerri, I will.'

'But I'm not there. Not at Roseleaf.'

'Monday. We'll be home on Monday. I'll ring you then.'

'I think you'll need to, once you have read my letter.'


## Annie Confesses

When she closed the garden gate behind her and turned to walk across the yard Kerri was surprised to see Macey emerging from the garage looking full of suppressed excitement. Damien was there, too, holding a large box.

She hadn't heard a car and was surprised to see Macey's red Mini in the yard. She should have been feeling elated because André also wanted to end things between them

110

but instead she felt sore and humiliated and wished she could escape to the cottage without being seen. There was so much to come to terms with here. She took a deep breath and tried to concentrate on the present.

'The silver jugs?' she said.

'I've got the makings here for a home-cooked meal to celebrate,' Damien said. 'We'll be concocting something tasty in about an hour, won't we, Macey?'

She dimpled up at him.

'If you say so, Damien.'

'We left the jugs at the auction house in Rollstone, Kerri,' he said sounding confident. 'That's where we've been. They're going to slot them in at the end of the auction on Saturday for us as a special favour to Macey.'

'Such a helpful man,' Macey said complacently.

'Too bad we didn't have time to sort the two remaining boxes still up there in the loft,' Damien said. 'More treasure, who knows? But this will do for a start.'

'And a good one,' Macey added.

Damien smiled at her, crinkling his eyes, and for a moment Kerri had the strange feeling that she wasn't here with them, but still at the top of the garden looking out over the reservoir and that the last half hour hadn't happened.

He seemed suddenly to realise that Kerri was present, too.

'Are you OK, Kerri? You look odd.'

She blinked.

'You said us.'

'Us?'

'You said the auctioneer is slotting the jugs in for us.'

'Of course it's for us,' Macey said. 'We're hoping for a huge result. He seemed to think we'd get one, didn't he?'

He nodded.

'Great, isn't it? Macey thinks it's going to set her up for the rest of her life. She's got big plans.'

He sounded as if he hoped they included him and Kerri felt a huge sinking of her heart. Her thumb would soon be better and she could drive away, collect her gear from Roseleaf and be free to live where she liked. Back in Cornwall at Damien's flat taking over the shop for him would be helpful if she had nowhere else to go.

The prospect filled her with gloom.

'Annie got you home in one piece, then?' Damien said cheerfully.

'Not Annie,' Kerri said.

'Then who?'

'We met Leo in Rawthwaite.'

'Leo?' Macey said her face immediately clouding.

'We had coffee and something to eat,' Kerri said immediately on the defensive. 'After I'd been to the hospital, that is. Leo thought I should go back today and let them take a look at my thumb.'

'So what did they say?' Damien asked.

'They drained it and put another dressing on. They seemed worried. I've got to go back again tomorrow. They said they might have to remove the nail.'

'That's terrible!' Damien looked shocked.

Macey sniffed.

'And then what? Where did you go then?'

'Down by the river, that's all.'

'Well, don't expect Leo to drive you about the countryside tomorrow. He's going to be here loading up the van for us for the car boot sale at Alderbeck. It's arranged isn't it, Damien?'

He nodded, his mind obviously on other things.

'So Leo knows you've got that lined up for him?' Kerri asked and then bit her lip. What was she thinking of to confront Macey in this way?

'I think I know Leo's wishes better than anyone,' Macey snapped. 'And don't forget it.'

'I won't.'

Macey looked at her suspiciously.

'What is that supposed to mean?'

But Kerri didn't want to be on the receiving end of an interrogation. She turned away. She had a lot to think about and needed the seclusion of the cottage.

Early next morning she heard sounds of

113

Damien stirring and lay listening as he went downstairs. She heard the kitchen door open and then shut. He obviously had planned to get started on transporting all the car boot items to the yard ready for loading. She wouldn't distract him even though she was wide awake after what seemed like a sleepless night. She wondered what time Leo would get here.

Her thumb was throbbing again in spite of the tablets she had been given and this in itself was worrying. Her mind too, had whirled with memories of her time at Roseleaf Nursery Gardens from the moment she started there until she left for her weekend in Cornwall.

André had gone off to Switzerland the week before full of his climbing holiday plans with his old school friends that didn't include her. She hadn't minded at the time but now she wondered if, unconsciously perhaps, he had felt relief at this opportunity to be apart for a while and he, like her, was beginning to question whether their plans for their future together were not the right way forward.

He would receive her letter soon, all being well. And he would be sure to phone again. They had been a couple for too long to part in this offhand way and it wouldn't seem right to either of them, especially as the decision was mutual. She felt bereft now that she was on her own. But that was stupid.

She threw back the duvet and got out of

114

bed, careful not to jar her bandaged thumb that might send a spasm of pain through her. She had always liked action and today would be no different.

First, though, she would phone Annie and ask her to drive her down to the hospital if she was free to do so. She dare not think, even for a moment, that her attraction to Leo was deeper than mere gratitude for his kindness to her. Avoiding a meeting with him was a sensible option when she was aware of how much she longed to be with him again.

She checked her watch. Lucy wouldn't have left for school yet, and with luck she could catch her before she set out.

The autumn air felt fresh as Kerri slipped out of the cottage. Moments later she was climbing up the steep garden path to where she knew she could get a signal. She still felt in desperate need of understanding and sympathy even after hours of coming to terms with the break-up with André. As usual, Lucy didn't fail her.

Then she rang Annie.

'No problem,' came her cheerful voice. 'I'll be with you about half nine.'

'I'll walk along to meet you,' Kerri said hastily.

'Understood. See you!'

That done, Kerri returned to the cottage, aware that it was a quarter to nine already.

Over at the house Damien was at the

breakfast table.

'Macey's busy somewhere,' he said.

They cleared away afterwards and then Kerri set out. She crossed the bridge and started out along the lane but hadn't gone far when she saw the grey car she knew was Annie's driving slowly along towards her. There was a handy turning space and Annie managed to position her car where she wanted it without too much to-ing and fro-ing.

She leaned across and opened the passenger door for Kerri.

'Great to see you,' she said.

Kerri smiled as she got in beside her.

'Not half as great as me seeing you.'

She was surprised to see another car coming up behind them. Annie gave it a wave and the occupants waved back.

'You know them?'

'Part of the team,' Annie said as they set off. 'Doing a stint in the bird hide.'

'They haven't been there all night!'

'From the early hours anyway. Dad's due to do an hour or two very soon. We might meet him.'

Kerri was glad they didn't because the lane was narrow.

This time Annie drove into the hospital car park and was early enough to secure a parking space without difficulty.

'I'll get us a coffee from the machine,' she said as they entered the building. 'Could be a

116

long wait.'

Kerri was afraid of that, knowing that Annie must be back at twelve, and had noted some taxi firms' phone numbers in a notice on the wall. She would never be able to repay Annie for her kindness and practical help but at least she wasn't going to get her into trouble with Max, who sounded a real ogre.

Annie placed the polystyrene mugs of coffee on the low table at Kerri's side.

'Too hot to touch at the moment,' she said.

Kerri checked that she had switched her mobile phone off as requested and laid it down on the table, too.

'You won't need that,' Annie said with confidence.

'I will later, to phone for a taxi if I'm not seen soon.'

'Who said? I've taken the morning off.'

'But it's Friday! You could be extra busy.'

Annie shrugged.

'So what? I owe you.'

'You owe me nothing, Annie.'

Annie was silent.

Kerri leaned back in her seat nursing her painful thumb. It was hard to think of anything else at the moment but the way the pain seemed to be spreading over her whole hand. She had drunk her coffee by the time she was called into the nurse-in-charge's room and the dressing removed.

'I think you should see the doctor again,' the

nurse said as she examined it. 'I'll see what I can do about that now.'

Another wait with a dressing loosely applied. This was tuning out to be more serious than Kerri thought and another draining took place. By the time she emerged it was well past eleven o'clock.

Annie jumped up in alarm when she saw her.

'You look like death,' she said.

'Thanks,' Kerri said faintly. 'They say it'll be OK but I must return every day. It's important. Otherwise it may get infected. They might have to take the nail off.'

'Come on, back to the car. You've got to be looked after. I'm not taking you back to that godforsaken place at Alder Knowle.'

Kerri tried to laugh.

'You said you want the cottage for your parents, that it sounds perfect!'

'Perfect for them to make their home. Not for you now, when you'll be on your own, with your brother and madam off elsewhere and not thinking of anything else.'

'If you say so.'

Annie caught hold of Kerri's arm and propelled her to the door.

'No arguments.'

'Where are we going?'

'To Mum and Dad's place. Dad'll be out doing his ornithology stuff but Mum'll feed us and look after you.'

Kerri was glad to let Annie take charge and leaned back in her seat, thankful she had found such a good friend. She closed her eyes as they left town and only opened them again when she felt the car turn off the main road.

'I thought you were asleep,' Annie said.

'Your driving was so smooth that I very nearly was,' said Kerri, sitting up and opening her eyes.

She expected Annie to laugh and was surprised when she looked at her and saw that she was frowning.

Once past the Old Oak she slowed the car down.

'What's wrong?'

'Don't you recognise where we are?'

'Of course. I'm getting to know the road quite well.'

'You'd think I'd know it well, too, wouldn't you? Well enough to know where it narrows?'

'Annie, what are you talking about?'

'Driving too fast, that's what. Taking the bend too fast and nearly sending an approaching car into the ditch.'

Suddenly light dawned.

'It was you!'

Annie stopped the car and yanked on the hand brake. She looked pale.

'Are you mad at me?'

She sat with her head bowed and her hands clasped together in her lap looking thoroughly dejected.

'I don't suppose you'll ever do it again,' Kerri said.

'Never,' Annie said fervently, raising her head so that Kerri saw the tears brimming in her eyes. 'I'm so sorry.'

'I think I know that. But the car's in one piece and nothing terrible happened.'

'Except for your thumb.'

'You've been so kind and helpful to me when I needed a friend here and didn't have one. What would I have done without you, Annie?'

'You wouldn't have needed to go to hospital, for a start.'

'There's no answer to that and I'm not going to think of one. Let's get going. It's best forgotten.'

'You're one in a million, Kerri.'

Annie looked a lot better now.

'Now you see why I needed to help you all I could.'

'You would have helped me anyway.'

'You think that's true?'

'Drive,' Kerri said. 'Or I'll get out and walk.'

Annie did as she was told and a few minutes later had pulled up outside a large stone house.

'Here we are. Mum knows I might be bringing you.'

Annie's mother was like an older version of her daughter and as friendly. She came forward at once as Annie ushered Kerri to the

120

back of the house and into the huge kitchen where copper pots hung from the ceiling and the smell of simmering lamb made Kerri's mouth water.

'Mary Brownley,' she said, taking Kerri's uninjured hand in hers and pressing it warmly. 'Annie has told me all about you. Come along in. Lunch is ready.'

'Dad still manning the bird hide?'

'He's been there since ten o'clock this morning.'

Mary Brownley talked gently as she served a meal that was easy to eat with one hand and Kerri felt relaxed.

Afterwards she and Annie washed up, with Annie doing the bulk of the work but Kerri helping by doing what she could. Annie made coffee and they settled down on reclining chairs in the garden. She was a good listener and Kerri found her worries about Damien came pouring out and Annie's interest and sympathy made Kerri feel better.

'Tell me, what is Lucy like?' Annie asked with a smile. 'Hard-hearted and cruel?'

'Not a bit of it.'

'Turning down a nice guy like Damien? It's hard to believe.'

'You sound as if you fancy him yourself.'

'Too young for me.'

'I've turned down a nice young chap, too,' Kerri confessed. 'So I must be hard-hearted and cruel.'

'Tell me all.'

And Kerri did, or as much as she thought necessary. When she had finished she sat in silence waiting for Annie's condemnation which didn't come.

'It happens,' Annie said. 'And you don't seem shattered by it, do you? And you could say it was a joint decision from what you said. You don't need to beat yourself up about it, Kerri. Tell me more about Lucy.'

Kerri smiled.

'We've known each other for years and get on so well, though we're not a bit alike.'

Annie screwed up her nose and gazed at Kerri speculatively.

'Let me guess. She's blonde and three feet tall . . .'

Kerri giggled and almost spilt her coffee. She put it down hastily on the low stone wall near her.

'You're crazy.'

'You said you're not a bit alike.'

'I didn't mean like that. The blonde bit's true and she's not very tall. Lucy's kind and gentle. She's got this calm personality and a sort of quiet courage you wouldn't expect. And she'd do anything for you.'

'And Damien was devastated.'

'He was at the time.'

'But now?'

'You've seen him with Macey.'

Annie frowned.

'Well, no, I haven't. You'll have to tell me.'

It was good to talk about it and get Annie's take on the situation. As Kerri expected, Annie was scathing about Macey's deliberate monopoly of Damien and her side-lining of Kerri.

'So what are they doing today?' she said.

'Sorting out the car boot things for tomorrow and getting Leo to help load it all in a van he can use.'

'Fascinating stuff. Do I hear a note of longing in your voice at the thought of all that hard work?'

Kerri felt warmth flood her face.

'Hardly, with only one useful hand.'

'I expect Leo Johnstone wishes you were there.'

'Leo?'

Annie indicated the garden fence with a nod of her dark head.

'He lives next door.'

'He does?' Kerri's heart leaped. She had known that Leo's home was somewhere in Alderfield but not where.

'Macey got her claws into him straight away and won't let go,' Annie said. 'He's a nice chap, Leo, and deserves better. And so does my brother, if he only had the sense to see it.'

Kerri finished drinking her coffee and leant back in her seat. The throbbing in her thumb had faded to a dull ache now.

'It was a wonderful meal,' she said. 'Your

123

mother is as kind as you are, Annie.'

'I'm not kind. I told you. It's only because I owe you. Nothing personal at all.'

'We've been there already, Annie. I'm in your debt and I don't forget it.'

'You could do something for me, if you like.'

Kerri looked at her enquiringly and Annie grinned back at her, pleading.

'I haven't had a look round your cottage yet.'

'With Macey in the offing?'

'We could check. You'll get a signal here. Phone the house and see if they're still around?'

'Why not? Do you know the number?'

'I soon will.' Annie leaped up. 'Stay there. I'll be back.'

Phoning the house wouldn't be much use if Macey and Damien were still in the yard and couldn't hear the house phone, Kerri thought. But Annie was back now and there was no harm in trying or in storing it on her mobile either.

That done she tried Damien's phone. No answer there. She clicked off after leaving a message on voicemail to report on her thumb.

'That's all right then,' Annie said cheerfully. 'The coast is clear.'

'If you like living dangerously.'

Annie giggled.

'I do!'

# Accused!

Kerri couldn't follow Annie's reasoning but didn't argue. It was time she got back anyway and there would be no harm in making sure that they would have Alder Knowle to themselves as Annie was so keen to see the property. She could just drop her off if there was a problem.

As they turned into Macey's track they saw a car approaching and Annie moved into the side.

'That's Dad,' she said.

He drew level and wound down his window. His likeness to his daughter was apparent in his smile and the shape of his face, Kerri thought as Annie introduced them. There were others in the car, too.

'Plenty going on there today,' he told them. 'We were just about to leave when a couple of rock pipits showed up.'

'Rock pipits?' Annie said incredulously. 'So far from the coast? I don't believe it.'

'That's what we thought they were, at first.'

'How come?'

'Unlikely, of course, so far from the coast.'

'You're just having a laugh,' Annie accused.

He smiled and winked at Kerri.

'Now would I do that? Although occasionally rock pipits do turn up at inland reservoirs.'

'But not so far from the coast as here.'

'These were meadow pipits, as we soon realised by the lighter colour of their legs. Smaller, of course, and their song is different. More of a high piping call and not as loud as the rock pipit, because it doesn't have to compete with the crashing surf. They stayed around for quite a while. That's why we're later than we intended.'

'Ha, any excuse to stay a bit longer.'

'We waited until they flew off.'

'They could return,' Annie said.

Her father shrugged.

'They could indeed. But I've got some lost property to report. We'll get one or two others of the ornithology group organised about these meadow pipits. It'll create a lot of interest. See you later.'

'Dad leads an exciting life,' Annie commented as they drove off. 'Rock pipits indeed.'

'We see rock pipits on the beach at home,' Kerri said. 'Running about on the hard sand between the rock pools at low tide and perching on rocks.'

'Lucky Dad sighting some meadow pipits,' Annie said. 'We haven't seen them here before.'

They crossed the stone bridge and as she drove past the open gateway Kerri checked that the yard was empty.

126

'All clear,' she said. 'Who's to say you're not just here to visit the bird hide anyway? Not even Macey could object to that.'

'Right,' Annie said. 'You're on.'

She parked in a suitable place and they got out. It was obvious that there was no one at home but to make quite sure she checked the garage door and found it unlocked. No vehicle was hiding away inside.

She smiled as Annie came creeping furtively into the yard looking to left and right in an exaggerated manner. 'Stop fooling,' she said. 'We're on a serious mission.'

'Mum and Dad would agree with you there,' Annie agreed. 'Lead on, Kerri, I simply can't wait.'

Kerri liked Annie's parents and hoped they would soon find a smaller property locally to suit them. It could be Macey's cottage, of course, if Annie approved of it.

And it seemed she did.

'Wow!' Annie said as they went in and she saw the kitchen with its yellow fitted cupboards and cream marble work tops.

'The sitting-room's not huge.'

'But a good square shape,' Annie said, following her in. 'And they might be able to put a conservatory on at the back. Lovely view of the reservoir. Dad'll like that.'

'Upstairs now?'

Annie went ahead this time and stopped in the doorway of the room to the right where

Kerri's camp bed in the middle of it looked lonely.

'Great,' Annie said in admiration. 'It's a good size and there's an excellent fitted wardrobe. Mum and Dad's room, of course, looking out over the reservoir.'

Kerri smiled.

'You've got it all planned.'

'And why not? Think positive, I say.' Annie went across the small landing to the second bedroom which also met with her approval as did the bathroom.

They went downstairs.

'My turn to make coffee for you. Or tea?'

'Neither.' Annie moved towards the door. 'You look all in, Kerri. My fault. I shouldn't have kept you so long. You need to get your head down on that flimsy-looking camp bed for a bit, instead of listening to me prattling on.'

'Sorry,' Kerri said apologetically. 'I'm grateful to you, Annie, truly.'

'I'll be in touch,' Annie replied. 'And don't forget I'm at your service for hospital duty whenever needed. See you!'

And she was gone. But not for long. Kerri heard the raised voices a moment or two later and rushed to the door to see what was going on outside. Macey had parked her car just inside the gateway blocking the entrance and had got out to confront an unwanted visitor.

Annie, her temper obviously at boiling

128

point, was giving as good as she got.

Kerri rushed to join them.

'This is your doing,' Macey stormed, turning to her. 'I can see your game, getting her here because she's after your brother. That's only too plain.'

'But . . .'

'And you needn't deny it.'

'Rubbish!' Annie cried.

Taken aback, Kerri could only stare.

Damien burst out of the car.

'What's going on?' he cried.

Suddenly Annie laughed.

'I'm old enough to be Damien's mother. Well, almost, given a few years. Cradle-snatching's neither for me, nor for you either, Macey Treghennel, whatever you're trying to bring off.'

Macey's face reddened and her eyes blazed.

'Get out!'

'I'll go when I'm good and ready. In any case, Damien's not interested in me and not in you, either. There's someone else . . .'

Macey sprang at her but Damien jumped between them. He looked pale and shaken as he tried to pull Macey away.

'No way will your parents get their hands on my cottage after this, Annie Brownley,' Macey spat out.

'Come on, Annie,' Kerri said, urging her away from the confrontation that had turned so ugly.

'No, wait, I'll . . .'

'No, Annie, no!'

Kerri held on tightly until she felt Annie relax. Damien was attending to Macey who now leaned against him, her head pressed into his chest. Kerri took advantage of the lull and together she and Annie squeezed past the car in the entrance.

'Now I've done it,' Annie moaned as they walked further along the track to where her car lay hidden. 'I should have had more sense than to think I could get a sneak preview of the cottage. Now Charles will hear of this. He'll kill me.'

'You said he always managed to get what he wants,' Kerri reminded her.

'Not this time.'

'How can you be sure?'

'He got her to agree to a sale yesterday evening. They went to this classy place at Rollstone. That's why I didn't want her to see me this morning. He warned me. And now I've ruined everything.'

Kerri leaned on Annie's car when they reached it. She was still shaking from the encounter.

Seeing this, Annie looked alarmed.

'I've got you involved in this, and now look at you, as white as a sheet.'

Kerri sat down suddenly on a protruding stone at the base of the wall.

'I feel involved already,' she said. 'Macey

130

takes every advantage to cross me in any way she can. This is because of me, you see, Annie.'

Annie gave a hoarse laugh.

'The woman's mad. I don't like leaving you here in her clutches.'

Kerri's smile was the best she could manage but she was feeling stronger now. She got up and glanced down at her bandaged thumb.

'I can cope, Annie. And I'll take up Leo's offer to drive me to the hospital tomorrow.'

'Unless our crazy friend has other plans for him.'

But Kerri wouldn't think of that at the moment. She had money now she had been to the bank and there were taxis.

Annie looked at her anxiously.

'You're feeling better now?'

'I'll phone you.'

Annie gave her a quick hug and got into her car. She wound down her window. 'Don't forget that phone call. I need to know she hasn't eaten you for supper.'

Kerri laughed as Annie drove away. Then she stood for a moment looking down over the intervening rough ground to the reservoir. She wondered if those meadow pipits were still in the vicinity. The bird hide was so well-camouflaged she could hardly pick it out and she marvelled that Annie's father and the other ornithologist could happily spend four hours in there.

She walked slowly back to the yard. Damien

131

and Macey had gone indoors, most likely to the house and she had better find them.

The back door of the house was unlocked and as Kerri slipped inside she heard voices in the hall and the slamming down of the telephone receiver. She braced herself as the door burst open and Macey erupted before her.

Damien, following her, looked perturbed.

'Bad news?' Kerri said through dry lips.

'The worst.' Macey threw herself down on a chair at the table and put her head in her hands. Her shoulders in her yellow shirt looked vulnerable.

Damien made a move forward but then thought better of it. He looked at Kerri with an anxious expression in his eyes.

'What is it?'

'One of the silver jugs is missing,' he said.

For a moment she could make no sense of his words and looked at him in surprise.

'Missing?'

'Yes, missing,' Macey said raising her head. 'The set is not complete. That little jug you were looking at? It's gone. Stolen. So, Kerri, tell us what you know about it.'

'Me?'

'Yes, you.'

'That was the auction house on the phone,' Damien elaborated. 'They unpacked the box and have found four jugs only. Unless we get the missing jug to them at once they are going to remove them from the sale.'

'But . . .'

He shrugged.

'We have to locate it.'

'Where is it, then?' Kerri said, confused.

'Yes, where is it, Kerri?' Macey jumped up and sent the chair crashing. 'Tell us that. What have you done with it?'

Kerri was horrified.

'You can't think . . .'

'Why not? You were there when Damien packed the jugs into the box. You can't deny that.'

'Wait a minute, Macey,' Damien cried, perturbed. 'You've got that wrong. Kerri would never steal anything.'

Kerri could see doubt forming in Damien's mind by the way he twisted his hands together as he looked at her quickly and then away again. The three of them had been present when the box was packed. The auction house could hardly be accused of raiding it.

'You can't possible think that of me, Damien!'

He looked unhappy.

'Of course I don't.'

'I'll phone Leo,' Macey said. 'He'll come and support me, and help me get to the bottom of it.'

Damien nodded. When she had left the room he looked at Kerri anxiously.

'You handed it to me, didn't you? The small

silver jug?'

'You think I didn't?'

'Just making sure.'

'I saw you wrap it in tissue paper and put it in the box. It was the first thing you put in.'

'So someone took it out again.'

'But not me.' Suddenly a wave of dizziness swept over her and blindly she felt for a chair and sank down on to it. She longed for Leo to be here and yet was glad he wasn't. More explanations, more interrogations . . . it was all beginning to feel too much to cope with.

Macey was back now.

'Leo's coming immediately. I knew he would. He knows how serious this is. I'll meet him in the car to save time. Coming, Damien? We can put him in the picture as we come along. He'll know what to do.'

But Damien shook his head.

'I'll wait here.'

She shot him a suspicious look, then smiled.

'Don't go away. We won't be long.'

'I wish we'd never come here!' Kerri cried.

'The auction means so much to Macey. She's relying on a good result and a good bit of profit from the car boot sale as well. There's lots of stuff.'

Kerri knew that already.

'I've finished with André,' she said abruptly.

Damien looked at her as if he didn't know what she was talking about.

'What's that you're saying?'

134

'And he with me. André. We're finishing. I told you.'

'You've told him now?

She nodded.

'We've still got to talk.'

'But you don't need to get back straight away?'

Kerri looked down at her thumb.

'I can't, can I, with this?'

'Still painful?'

'A bit.'

She raised her head as Leo came in, cheered at seeing him. She stood up, and tried to smile.

'So what's going on?' he said.

'I told you, Leo.' Macey sounded put out.

He ignored her.

'How come there's something missing from the box Damien packed up yesterday afternoon?' He was looking at Kerri, his eyes seeming to see right through her.

She cleared her throat, feeling a stir of guilt as if she really had sneaked one of the jugs out of the box and had packed it away safely in her bag. It would almost be a relief to admit that she had done it, and not have to face a lot of questioning and suspicion. How stupid was that?

She stared right back at him and held her head high.

'Macey thinks you can solve the problem for her.'

'I'm not a magician.'

135

Not in that sense perhaps, she thought, but he was doing strange things to her heart that seemed to be beating so quickly she thought it would burst.

'Damien wouldn't have bothered stealing it,' Macey pointed out. 'He's an antique expert, for goodness' sake.'

'And?'

'He refused to accept one when I offered it to him, so why would he need to steal it? That only leaves Kerri.'

'Unless, of course, thieves broke in to the auction house overnight and selected one of the jugs to carry off with them?' Leo suggested.

Macey looked scornful.

'That's not possible.'

'A bit of a dark horse then, are you, Kerri?' Leo said.

'I don't like being accused of something I didn't do.'

'We've only got your word you didn't.'

'And only Macey's that I did.'

He nodded.

'You have a point there. Presumably all three of you saw the jugs being packed into the box? And you went with them to the auction house in Rollstone this morning?'

'Well, yes,' Damien said. 'To get them there for the Saturday auction tomorrow. Macey drove, of course. There was a bit of a fuss going on when we arrived about something

136

or other. They said they'd get back to us later today. It was a late entry, you see. I think some mistake was made somewhere. Kerri's not a thief.'

'I'm not standing here a moment longer listening to this,' Kerri said.

A ringing of the front door bell made her jump.

'Who's that at this time?' Macey demanded.

'Better go and see,' Leo said mildly.

It was too much to expect that the missing jug should have turned up on the doorstep, Kerri thought, but if it had it wouldn't have had such a deep voice as the person she could hear talking to Macey in the hall.

They spoke for a few minutes and then Macey returned to the kitchen looking flustered.

'It's Charles Brownley,' she said. 'He needs to speak to me. Get this sorted out, please, Leo.' She left.

Leo shrugged his shoulders.

'Macey's phoned the police, I take it?'

'Well, no,' Damien said. 'The auction people said they would be doing that if it doesn't turn up here.'

'How do you know that that's what the auction house said?' Kerri asked suddenly. 'Who answered the phone?'

'Macey, of course.'

She said nothing but she was thinking hard.

'I don't see why Macey thinks I could do

137

anything to help matters,' Leo said.

'And I'm not standing for it,' Kerri said. 'I'm off.'

She yanked so hard at the back door handle that it nearly came off in her hand. She was aware of Leo looking at her but it was Damien who followed her and caught her up as she reached the door into the walled garden.

'Leo said to say goodnight, Kerri,' he said. 'No need to go storming off like this.'

'Every need. Are you coming or not?'

The door banged shut behind him and in silence he followed her up the garden.

'Macey's under a lot of stress,' he said breathing hard.

She swung round.

'So that makes it all right to accuse me of stealing, does it, Damien?'

'I know you wouldn't do it, Kerri. I said so.'

'Not convincingly enough.'

'Please, Kerri, try to understand.'

'Understand what?' she cried, waving her bandaged hand at him. 'What about *my* stress?'

'But you're different, Kerri, stronger and more able to cope.'

'Not this time.'

Damien looked alarmed.

'What are you going to do?'

'I can't stay here after this.'

'You'd go? But how? And it any case it would look as if you were guilty. You don't

138

want that, do you, Kerri?'

She was pulled up short at that. She was stuck here, well and truly, and she couldn't do a thing about it.

Suddenly she flopped down against the wall and bowed her head. Frustrated tears sprang to her eyes, and she let them overflow.

## In The Bird Hide

Kerri spent a restless night. Her bandaged thumb was uncomfortable in whatever position she lay on her narrow camp bed. At last she got up, slung her jacket on top of her nightdress and padded across to the window to gaze down at the reservoir gleaming in the moonlight.

A pearly glow hung over everything and it was beautiful. The peace of the garden earlier had got to her through her storm of weeping and for a little while she had felt released of something that had lain dormant since their arrival. And sorry, too, for her poor brother who hadn't known what to do to help her. At last she had scrubbed at her eyes, got to her feet and apologised.

'It's OK,' Damien had said awkwardly.

He hadn't seen her cry since they were children, and she had lost her temper over being accused of something of which she was innocent, some little thing like breaking the handle off an old tea cup that didn't matter anyway.

But this accusation was deeply serious and she didn't know what she could do about it. How did you prove you hadn't done something unless you had an alibi? And none of them had that.

She thought of Leo and the way he had looked at her as they had argued about the missing jug with increasing amounts of suspicion that had led nowhere. All the time she had felt guilty because of Macey's accusation as if somehow this meant she must be at fault. Stupid, she knew, but she hadn't been able to help it.

Charles Brownley had long gone when she and Damien returned to the house leaving Macey tight-lipped and furious. No easy forgiveness for Annie there, Kerri thought. She wondered briefly what part Leo was expected to play since he hadn't been involved at the start. He had taken it with surprising composure as he accepted whatever role Macey assigned to him.

A scratch meal of bread and cheese had been eaten at the kitchen table but no-one was hungry. Afterwards they pushed what was left to one side and continued sitting there for what seemed hours to Kerri who was longing to escape to the cottage. She glanced at Damien once or twice and saw that he was feeling the same by the way he was trying to disguise yawns every now and again.

At last Leo glanced at his watch.

'This won't do,' he said as he got up and stretched. 'An early start in the morning, Macey. The car boot sale, remember?'

'It's no longer important,' she said. 'I'm not interested.'

'You have to be. Don't forget it's Saturday tomorrow. The van's over at Alderbeck fully loaded as you know, and it can't stay like that.'

Macey shrugged.

'We need to go the auction house, Damien and me,' she said. 'And I wanted you there, too, Leo.'

For a moment Leo seemed at a loss. Then he glanced at Kerri.

'Could you give me a hand at Alderbeck instead, Kerri?'

She looked up in surprise.

'I've only one hand available. And my dressing needs to be changed on the other.'

'I'll run you in to Rawthwaite afterwards.'

There was nothing Macey could say to that but she threw Kerri a look of dislike.

'I suppose that will have to do,' she said grudgingly.

'That's it then,' Leo said. 'I'll pick you up at seven in the morning, Kerri.'

Now, Kerri glanced at her watch. Five-thirty. The moonlight still illuminated everything outside but now it seemed to shine

141

with a golden light, because in just an hour and a half she would be seeing Leo again, even though he had looked pale and stern most of the time they had been talking. He hadn't looked at her once during the raging discussion, as if he were deeply concerned that there might be a grain of truth in Macey's accusations. Damien, too, had been subdued.

But today was a new day and she was spending part of it with Leo. Surely he wouldn't have suggested that, if he really thought she was guilty of lying and stealing? Unless, of course, he intended using the time to make her confess where she had hidden the object that had assumed such significance?

\*        \*        \*

The field belonging to Alderbeck House that had been allocated to the car boot sale was on the opposite side of the road from the house and was already seething with activity when Leo and Kerri arrived.

'I've never been to one of these before,' she said, marvelling that it wasn't yet eight o'clock in the morning.

The sun was only just rising above the steep hill to the east and there were long shadows across the grass. The air smelt of damp earth and engine fumes. The van Leo had used to transport their goods for sale was parked in a sunny spot against the drystone boundary wall.

142

She saw that a couple of folded trestle tables obviously allocated to them were leaning against it.

'We'll soon have those covered,' Leo said.

He caught hold of one and with a flick of his wrist got it up and into position. Another moment and the other one was up too. He opened the back door of the van and revealed several large boxes and many bulging bags of assorted sizes.

Kerri felt a moment of panic.

'I'm not going to be much use at this,' she said apologetically.

Leo pulled out a laden box and placed it to one side of the tables.

'Don't worry, you'll be fine as soon as we get started,' he said. 'I'll deal with emptying all this but you can help if you like. And you could be useful arranging some of it on the tables as you think fit. And then the fun will start.'

'Fun?'

'In an hour's time this place will be heaving.'

'I thought it was heaving now!'

'Not yet with customers,' he said. 'All these people are like us, setting up their stalls. You'll be needed when things get started, believe me.'

'But how much do we charge for it all?'

'You make instant decisions and then get what you can. How are your bargaining skills?'

'Bargaining? It can't be as bad as all that.'

'Wait and see.'

He now had a pile of boxes out of the van. She tried to move one and its weight surprised her. Leo made it look so easy, she thought, as she opened the top and removed some articles wrapped in newspaper.

Carefully, she unwrapped them. This was a box of unwanted china, some of it prettily patterned with flowers and leaves. She placed them at one side of the first table. By the time the van was empty even Leo looked slightly flushed with his exertions.

He flicked back his hair as he smiled at her. He looked so handsome in his navy jersey that her heart seemed to miss a beat.

'What's wrong?' he said.

She smiled.

'What could be wrong on such a lovely morning?'

'I can think of a few things.'

So could Kerri but she wasn't going to dwell on them.

'We haven't got room for all the stuff,' she said.

'Not to worry. We can replenish as things get sold. Here's the first of our customers, hopefully.'

He smiled at the girl coming towards them so devastatingly that Kerri thought she might be captivated. But she had eyes only for a teapot in the shape of a thatched cottage.

'How much?' she demanded.

Kerri took a deep breath.

144

'It's a good make.'

'A fiver?' The girl held out a note.

'Six pounds,' Kerri said firmly.

'Five-fifty.'

'Only if you've got the exact money.'

The girl produced the coins and went away satisfied.

'Well done,' Leo said. 'I'd have asked for three.'

'Would you really?' She felt anxious.

'Only joking. This is a mug's game. We get what we can, win some, lose some. Macey doesn't want any of it back so we must get rid of the lot.'

By the end of the morning most of it was gone and Kerri felt exhausted. Only the contents of one box was left. Leo tipped them out on the table with care and looked at the objects critically.

'What a shame there isn't another silver jug here to replace the one that was lost,' he said.

Kerri stared down at the assortment in front of them. One or two little white china jugs were among them with pictures of birds on them. Attractive in their own way. Macey's grandfather must have thought so. What a shame that she didn't want to keep them. One of them had a pair of robins on them, another a blackbird and a couple of others had ducks of a kind she had never seen before. She picked one up to look at it more closely.

A flash of illumination hit her with such

145

suddenness for an electrifying moment she felt odd. Her memory jolted and in her mind's eye she saw Annie's father slowing his car and drawing up beside Annie's vehicle as they drove back to Alder Knowle on the track alongside the reservoir. Something about a pipit, rare in these parts, a meadow pipit. And some lost property he was on his way to report to the police that he and his fellow bird-watchers had found in the bird hide. Could it be?

Kerri stared at Leo in dawning comprehension.

'What's wrong?'

This was what had been niggling the back of her mind since yesterday! Kerri put the jug down on the table, aside from the others.

'I have to make a phone call. Now. Do you mind?'

She didn't wait for an answer but rushed off to find a quieter place, pulling her mobile out of her pocket as she ran.

Leo watched her go. She had looked desperate. An important phone call that couldn't wait? He wanted to sweep all that remained off the table, in the hope that the resulting crash would somehow ease his frustration. But these objects were Macey's property and as such must be treated with respect.

Just as he had always treated Macey with respect, on behalf of his father. It was an odd

146

situation and one that he had never considered before. What was it about Macey that drew people to her immediately and then, as time went on, repelled them with her desperation. Her vulnerability, he supposed, and a deep need for something she hadn't yet found. She needed a firm hand, someone to take charge of her life and stand no nonsense.

He took a deep breath, feeling totally out of his depth.

'How much is this lot, mate?'

Leo turned to see an elderly couple examining the remaining stock with interest. Hastily he picked up the duck-decorated jug.

'This one's already spoken for.'

'I'll take the rest off your hands for a couple of quid.'

Leo considered his offer. Well, why not? Macey had lost interest, after all, and they had done far better than he had expected.

He found an empty box from beneath the tables in which to load the things. Then he bundled up the money bags and locked them in the van for safety. The other boxes he flattened and loaded them in, too. He'd dispose of them later in the recycling place in Rawthwaite after Kerri's hospital visit.

But where was she? There were no problems with lack of mobile phone signals here, so she wouldn't have had far to go. He wondered about this important phone call that seemed couldn't wait and wished he'd asked more about it. But what business was it of his what phone calls Kerri made? Still, she had looked desperate and he felt in some way responsible for her well-being.

He needed to return the van to base and collect his own car. This wouldn't take long. Maybe a note left on the table to say where he was and asking her to remain there until he returned would be a good idea.

That sorted out, he drove off across the bumpy field keeping a look-out in case she was on her way back.

*     *     *

Annie wasn't answering her mobile. Kerri, frustrated, tried three times with suitable gaps in between, in case she had got her number wrong. The third time she left a voicemail message in the hope that Annie would get back to her as soon as possible.

The field was emptying fast and Leo would want to clear up. She started to walk back past the dismantled stalls, dodging the piles of goods lying about among them, until she reached the spot where the van should had been parked and their stall set up.

The note attached to one of the folded tables said that Leo would be straight back. From where?

She pulled out her mobile again and stared at the blank screen.

Annie, where are you when I need you?

At her parents' home? Their number was stored in her contacts list. Hopefully, she clicked on it and listened to the ringing tone. It cut off and a recorded message told her that they would get back to her as soon as they could. No doubt Annie's father was hidden away in that bird hide with his bird-watching mates hoping more meadow pipits would turn up and not thinking at all of the silver jug he had found the day before.

If it was the silver jug . . .

The toot of a car horn made her jump and she saw Leo's car driving across the grass towards her. She ran towards it.

'You found my note, then?'

She nodded.

'Get in,' he said as he leaned across to open the door for her. You didn't think I'd go off without you?'

'It's not that. I've been trying to get hold of Annie.'

'Annie? Annie Brownley?'

'I need to ask her something. She's not answering her phone and her parents aren't at home.'

Leo paused with his hand halfway to releasing the hand brake.

'You're not making much sense here, you know, Kerri. You said you had an important phone call to make. Was it to Annie?'

Kerri nodded.

'Mr Brownley said he had some lost property to report to the police. I thought it might be the silver jug. I wanted to make sure.'

Leo let out a long whistle and turned off the ignition.

'When was this?'

'Yesterday. We met him. He had been in the bird hide. That's where he found something.'

'But it could have been anything. Something one of the other ornithologists forgot and left behind like a notebook of important sightings or binoculars.'

'I know. But why would he need to report those? Wouldn't he just notify the organiser of his local ornithologist group? And you know who that is. Annie! Wouldn't the rightful owner contact her, too? And if it wasn't claimed, then the police could be informed.'

'I see what you mean.' Leo looked thoughtfully at his hands on the steering wheel. 'You've thought this through.'

'Not really. It just came to me. Annie's father seemed to think it was important enough to be officially reported immediately. Isn't it too much of a coincidence to assume it was not the silver jug?'

'Right. We'll have to do the obvious and find out for sure. But not yet.'

The engine sprang to life.

'Where are we going?' she asked.

'Rawthwaite Hospital.'

She gaped at him.

'I'd forgotten. But we can't go now. Not when we have to know about the jug, for Macey's sake.'

'Of course now. At least, we'll grab a sandwich or something first and a cold drink and then head off.'

'But . . .'

'Don't argue, Kerri. You've been told to show up at the hospital today. They wouldn't have said that if it wasn't important.'

'But I need to know about the jug.'

'Not as much as you need to know you won't lose your thumb!'

She could see he meant what he said by the firm look about his mouth. She sank down in her seat and thought about it. She was surprised that Leo's reaction about the jug was so low key, almost as if it didn't really matter.

He slowed down as they reached the refreshment van and pulled up nearby. There were packets of cheese and salad sandwiches left. Leo bought two of them and a couple of cans of ginger beer.

When they eventually got to the hospital they had what seemed to Kerri a long frustrating wait because her mind was filled with the implications of what she suspected. The bird hide was such an odd place for a silver jug to turn up.

Someone would have put it there deliberately, but who could possibly have done such a thing?

Leo got up to get coffees from the machine and when he came back he smiled at her wryly.

'It's no good dwelling on it,' he said.

'How did you know I was?'

He sat down beside her and placed her coffee on a low table where she could reach it with her unbandaged hand.

'Easy. You've got that withdrawn look, as if you're miles away.'

'Sorry.'

'This is a bad business, Kerri. I don't know what to think.'

'Now you're dwelling on it,' she countered.

At that moment she was called in, so she didn't hear his response. But he looked thoroughly cast down as she glanced back at him. He was sitting with his hands clasped between his knees, staring at the floor.

The change of dressing made her thumb feel a little easier. And the swelling had gone down a little. The nurse made encouraging noises as she bandaged it again and Kerri felt heartened.

Leo was still staring into space when she rejoined him and wasn't aware of her approach at first.

'Leo?'

He looked up with a start.

She smiled.

'All done.'

'Feeling any better?' He got up.

'A little. Thanks for bringing me.'

'Let's go.'

'Silver jug time now?' she said as they reached the door. 'Are we calling at the police station?'

'Hardly. Macey will have to do the turning up and claiming it, with proof of who she is.'

'Well, yes. So where, then?'

'The Old Oak first. To see if Annie's still there. If not, the Brownleys' place, next door to mine. With luck they'll be home now. They'll tell us what the object was. Be prepared for a disappointment, though.'

'No need. Wait and see.'

'You sound very sure.'

'Even if it is Macey's lost silver jug it'll be too late for the auction, won't it?'

'More than likely.'

Outside, it had begun to rain, a thin drizzle that dampened everything. Leo's car was parked some way away and by the time they reached it their hair was covered in a fine mist.

'Lucky it wasn't like this earlier,' Kerri said.

She settled back in her seat thinking how deadened the countryside looked now. The mist was rolling down from the hills obliterating the water of the reservoir so that you would hardly know it was there.

The ground smelt of wet earth as they got out of the car outside the Old Oak.

'Not much activity here.' Leo pushed open the door.

Someone was polishing glasses at the bar, but it wasn't Annie.

'Not in till tonight,' she told them brusquely.

'So that's that.' Leo and Kerri went out into the damp afternoon again. 'Plan B it is.'

They hadn't far to go to pull up outside Leo's cottage. The house next door looked imposing in contrast to its smaller neighbour. They walked up the drive together and Kerri felt her heart beating extra fast. She didn't know if Leo's nearness was causing it, or her desperation to get at the truth and clear her name.

Leo rang the bell. It seemed ages before they heard the sound of approaching footsteps and the door was opened.

'Leo?' Annie's mother said with pleasure, 'And Kerri! Nice to see you again, dear.'

'Is Annie here, or Derek?' Leo asked.

'You've just missed him. What a shame. He's taking Buster for a walk and Annie went with him.'

'Will they be long?'

'I'm hoping they won't get carried away and forget that Derek and I are going off to Harrogate this evening. But of course Annie's got work to go to, so it should be all right. Max is so lenient with her, though, she often shows up late and not a word said, the naughty girl.'

Kerri was astonished.

'Lenient?'

'He's big softie. She leads him a bit of a

154

dance but he seems to like it.'

'So we might catch sight of them,' Leo pressed.

'We need to know something, you see,' Kerri said.

'Can I be of any help?'

Kerri glanced at Leo.

'Someone left something in the bird hide near Alder Knowle and it's important for us to know what it is.'

'Ah, that. Sadly I'm not at liberty to say what at the moment. Annie's orders, and I daren't disobey my daughter.'

Leo smiled.

'Best not. We'll catch Annie later if we don't see her now.'

Mrs Brownley smiled back.

'And the very best of luck.'


## Dinner With Leo

'It seems as if you're right and the silver jug may turn up safe and well,' Leo said as he put the car into gear and they set off again.

'It would be good to be sure.'

He drove slowly so they could keep a look-out for Annie and her father but there was no sight of them plodding home with the dog.

They found Macey and Damien in one of the outhouses at the back of the house. Both looked discouraged.

'We're going to get the two remaining boxes down and sort them out here,' Damien said. 'Then we can dispose of the stuff Macey doesn't want.'

'I can give you a hand with that,' Leo said. 'Another car boot sale?'

Macey shrugged.

'Who knows?'

'Don't you want to know how well we did today?'

'And we think we know where the lost jug is,' Kerri said.

Macey looked at her suspiciously.

'We? So you've actually told Leo what you did with it?'

Damien's eyes lit up.

'So where is it?'

'We have to check with Annie first to find out for sure if it's the lost jug. But we think it is.'

'Annie!' Macey spat out. 'That girl again. Why can't she keep her nose out of my business?'

'It's my business to clear my name,' Kerri said.

'And finding the jug would do that?'

Kerri hesitated, knowing she had a point. But at least her fingerprints wouldn't be on it? Or would they? She bit her lip, thinking about it. Damien had handed her the jug yesterday to look at it more closely after all.

'How much did you make at the sale?' Macey sounded suspicious, as if she thought they had squandered a good bit of it already.

'We did pretty well,' Leo said. 'Thanks to Kerri.'

Macey eyed Kerri's bandaged hand.

'Better now, is it?'

'Much better,' Kerri replied firmly although she wasn't too sure of how much.

'A slow job,' the nurse had said. 'And take it easy.'

'If you come into the kitchen we'll show you the result,' Leo said. 'Lead the way, Kerri.'

Macey hung back, saying she wanted to get a padlock from the garage to secure the outhouse door and promising to join them after that.

The pile of silver and copper Leo poured out on to the table from the containers looked impressive, and so did the wad of notes he produced from the inside pocket of his jacket. When he had checked there were none left he slung it over the back of a chair to dry and then tossed back his lock of loose hair.

Damien smiled at Kerri.

'Well done.'

'It was good,' she said. 'I'd do it again.'

'You might have to,' Damien told her. 'There's another one at Copplebeck sometime next week and we don't know what's in those boxes out there yet.'

'Will the silver jug be among the items?'

157

'What an idea!'

'Macey hasn't shown much interest in it,' Kerri said.

For a moment Damien looked confused but then his face cleared.

'I suppose she can't be sure it's hers until she goes to Rawthwaite to claim it.'

Kerri didn't bother to comment on that. Instead she took off her jacket, hung it on the hook on the back of the door and shook back her damp hair.

Leo took down a china bowl from the shelf and filled it with the loose cash, placed the notes on top and weighted them down with a couple of handy spoons.

He beamed round at them.

'I think this calls for a celebration, don't you? How about I take us all out to a meal at the Old Oak after we've got those boxes down from the loft?' He glanced at Macey as she came into the kitchen and smiled wryly. 'Paid for out of my own money, of course, Macey. A good idea?'

Kerri smiled but before she could say anything Macey moved over to where Damien stood leaning on the table and slid her arm through his.

'Not good. We've got other plans, haven't we, Damien?'

He hesitated, and Kerri knew he would have liked to accept Leo's invitation.

'We have?'

'Definitely.' Macey smiled at Leo, her dimples showing. 'Sorry, Leo. We'll get together and do that another night instead, shall we?'

'Just the two of us, then,' Leo said. 'So, how about that job you want doing, Damien? Then I'll get off and change out of these old things and be back for you at seven, Kerri? Is that all right?'

She smiled her acceptance, afraid to say anything in case a tremor in her voice gave her delight away.

She wished she had something more elegant to wear than her white sleeveless blouse with her spare jeans, and her antique silver and ruby pendant that André had given her for her birthday. It was the best she could do, and she hoped she didn't look too bad. She had had time for a shower so her hair was clean and shining.

While she waited for Leo she fingered her pendant, wondering what André was doing at this moment and what the girl he was bringing home with him was like. She would probably see for herself, because she would have to go back to Roseleaf to sort out her belongings and pack up everything that belonged to her. It had to be done, and sooner rather than later.

She glanced at her watch and as she did so she heard a car engine and Leo's Volvo swept into the yard and drew up outside the cottage. He leaned across and opened the passenger

159

door for her and then got out to close it behind her. He was wearing black this evening and it suited his fair good looks.

'All set?'

She saw a flicker of appreciation in his eyes as he smiled at her.

'Raring to go.'

The Old Oak was full to bursting point as it was Saturday evening and Kerri hesitated in the doorway, unable to see a spare seat anywhere. Something that smelled mouth-watering wafted across to them.

'A popular place,' she said, prepared to be disappointed.

But Leo had thought of that and there was a table for two tucked away in one corner out of sight of the door. As he led the way to it she saw the Reserved sign on it with relief.

'You think of everything,' she murmured.

They sat down and Leo leaned back in his seat to get a better view of the menu board on the wall.

'Can you see it all right, Kerri? What d'you fancy? Steak and kidney pie for me, I think.'

'I'd better go for shepherd's pie. Easier to eat with one hand. I like it, anyway.'

'And what to drink?'

'Lemonade shandy would be fine.'

Leo got up to go to the bar and Kerri saw that Annie and the girl they had seen earlier were totally absorbed in serving others and taking orders. Clearly he had no chance of

160

doing anything extra than to place their own when it was his turn.

'Annie will speak to us when she can,' Leo said, returning to their table with the drinks. 'The best I could do for the moment.'

This wasn't as long as Kerri feared because after Annie delivered two plates of fish and chips to the next table she paused by their own.

'Something important?' she said. She whipped her pad and Biro out her pocket and stood poised in an exaggerated stance. 'Out with it, then!'

'We'd better tell her quickly,' Kerri joked. 'Or she may not allow us anything to eat.'

Leo smiled.

'Go ahead, Kerri.'

'The lost property your father found in the bird hide on Thursday . . . can you tell us what it was, Annie?'

Annie narrowed her eyes in surprise.

'It belonged to you, did it? Why didn't you say so?'

'Because I hadn't lost anything. And we still don't know what it is. If it's what we suspect, it could be Macey's.'

'Macey Treghennel? Why was she in our bird hide?'

'Was it an engraved silver jug, Annie?'

'An odd thing to find there, don't you think?' Annie moved her weight from one foot to the other, obviously prepared for a long chat. 'Betty and Cliff were in residence in the hide until about nine. They'd been there all night. It wasn't there then.'

'Annie!'

Annie jumped to attention.

'I'll be back soon with your food,' she promised.

Leo raised his glass to his lips and then put it down again. His eyes shone in the light of the lamp hanging just above his head and he smiled.

'I would say that seems conclusive, wouldn't you?'

'It's a relief it's turned up.' She drank some of her shandy, feeling the cold liquid slide down her throat.

'The birdwatchers in the hide must have been keen, to have stayed there all night or at least from the early hours,' she said.

'Or mad.'

She wondered what they hoped to see, or hear. Nightjars or nightingales? She knew so little about birds that she didn't know if they could be heard around here at this time of year. She opened her mouth to ask Leo, and then thought of something.

'We met Annie's father in a car with two others on the way back yesterday,' she said.

'What time was that?'

About two, I think. Or maybe later. They said they'd been there since ten. Some others had been there at least since the early hours

162

till about nine.'

Leo picked up his glass and looked at it thoughtfully.

'So there was a one-hour slot for someone to hide it then. What were you doing during that time, Kerri?'

For a moment she couldn't speak for the realisation that he didn't trust her after all.

'What's wrong?'

She stared at him.

He must have realised how his comment sounded because he put his drink down and caught hold of her unbandaged hand in both of his.

'I'm not doubting you, Kerri, not for a moment. It's helpful to get the facts straight, that's all, so there's absolutely no doubt in anyone else's mind either. Believe me.'

Her heart leaped. Leo believed in her innocence! She smiled, feeling her face glow and as if a great heavy bundle had fallen from her shoulders.

'Even yesterday seems ages ago,' she said, wrinkling her brow in an effort to remember. 'We always go over to the house for breakfast, Damien and me . . .'

'What time would that be?'

'Just before nine. Macey wasn't there. Damien and I cleared away and washed up between us. It took ages because of my hand. I met Annie just by the bridge.'

Leo was looking solemn now, clearly

considering the implications but not yet ready to voice them.

'Macey must hate me more than I thought,' she said sadly.

He let a silence fall between them and she didn't attempt to break it. Instead she ran the fingers of her right hand round the edge of the table, feeling indents in the wood at intervals where something must have knocked into it.

Annie was back now with their food, the steam rising from the plates she set before them in a burst of delicious-smelling warmth. Afterwards Leo ordered apple-pie and custard for himself and crème caramel for Kerri.

The tables round them were emptying now and by the time they finished they were one of only three couples left in the room.

'Where is everybody?' Kerri said as Annie returned to remove their plates.

'There's a jazz concert down in Rawthwaite,' she said. 'Most of them were going there.'

Leo looked surprised.

'Tonight?'

'Didn't you know? Tickets have been on sale here all week. The last two went to Macey Treghennel. I thought you'd be there with her but I see you've better things to do.'

'She obviously had other plans.'

Annie flicked a look of enquiry at Kerri and then grinned as she collected up the pepper and salt and balanced them precariously at the side of the top plate.

'Damien has never liked jazz,' Kerri said.

Leo looked interested.

'And you?'

'I've never understood what it's all about.'

'Then it's time you did. And it's not too late now.'

'But the last tickets have been sold,' she pointed out.

'The two you had here to sell. Isn't that right, Annie? They'll have some to sell on the door.'

Annie winked at Kerri.

'Take him up on that, why don't you?' she said as she turned to leave them. 'Live dangerously.'

Kerri laughed, feeling lighthearted suddenly. She thought of Damien's high spirits when they were doing the washing up and then his swift change to seriousness again. Life was too short not to take advantage of anything on offer, so why not?

'Sounds good,' she said.

'You'll come?'

'Just try to stop me.'

Dark had fallen now but there was still enough light left to glimmer on the surface of the water as they drove down the Rawthwaite road alongside the reservoir.

'The moon will be up later,' Leo said.

Already there was a lightness in the sky to the east. Parking was easy outside the hall although many vehicles were already there.

Inside the building there was room to slip into the back row of seats as the six musicians came onto the stage and were introduced to their audience by a man in a black suit.

'Ladies and gentlemen, I give you . . . the Red Dervish!'

The applause was deafening.

At first, it seemed to Kerri like a muddle of strident sound, but after a while she appreciated the beat and rhythm she began to hear in it. She listened for clever improvisation in familiar tunes and found them.

Afterwards, Leo caught hold of her elbow and propelled her through the crush to the outside door. The moon had risen as he said it would. The clouds had rolled away and in its light she saw the enthusiasm shining in his eyes.

'Thanks for bringing me,' she murmured.

'You enjoyed it?'

She nodded. There was no doubt that he had and she was pleased. He deserved it after the hard work he had done on Macey's behalf today.

They saw that the car, when they reached it, was blocked in by a Land-Rover parked askew across the front and another in the way of that. Leo shrugged in resignation.

'This happens,' he said. 'We'll just have to wait.'

'How about I buy us a coffee at the place across the road?' she said. 'It's time I treated

166

you to something.'

He smiled.

'If you insist.'

From the window they had a clear view of the car park and it wasn't long before the offending vehicles were claimed and driven off. Even so Leo didn't seem anxious to move.

Kerri finished her coffee and looked at him enquiringly.

'Another?'

'Do you want to get back?'

'No,' she said. 'But they may wonder where I am.'

'I doubt that,' he said. 'Look out there.'

In the glow of the street light Kerri saw Macey, with her arm through Damien's, coming out of the hall. They were talking and laughing as they moved away along the street.

\* \* \*

Alder Knowle was in darkness as they drove into the yard. In the beam from the headlights the cobbles looked like trays of freshly baked buns in a cake shop window.

'Just as well I'm not hungry or I'd want to eat the lot,' she said aloud.

'What are you talking about?' Leo reversed the Volvo and pulled up outside the cottage with a squeak of brakes.

'Just a mad thought.'

'I've been having a few of those, too,' he

said. 'And I want a few answers to one or two questions. Like, why would Macey hide one of her own jugs when she needs the money the complete set would have fetched at auction?'

As he fell silent Kerri didn't reply but sat quietly, too, deep in thought.

'Because there's something she needs even more?'

'That's a deep thought. Where did that come from?'

She didn't know. But what other reason could there be?

Leo was silent again, absorbing this new idea.

'Why place the silver jug in the bird hide?'

'So it would be found by someone else?' Kerri suggested. 'And the blame placed on me.'

'She wanted to hurt you that much?'

'She wanted me out of the way.'

Damien had scorned this suggestion, and she thought Leo might do the same. She fumbled for the door handle with her good hand but he leaned across to prevent her.

'No hurry,' he said.

She turned towards him and even in the gloom she saw the intensity of his gaze. She couldn't move for the rush of longing that filled her. It seemed that the car was filled with brilliance and yet the moonlight outside cast only a silver light across the yard.

But suddenly the place was filled with noise,

168

other lights and the sound of voices as Macey's car swept in and pulled up beside Leo's. The moment had passed and Kerri was left feeling bruised and raw.

Leo was out at once and round at her side of the car opening the passenger door for her.

'We've got something to show you,' Macey said, her voice jubilant.

'Not tonight,' Leo said.

'Now!'

'It's late. I'll come back in the morning.'

'We had a look at the boxes in the outhouse before we left,' Damien explained. 'We've found some valuable items at last. Quite a lot! Macey's so excited she's been telling everybody.'

'We'll see them better in daylight,' Leo told him.

Damien nodded and yawned.

'It's been a long day.'

'And a longer one tomorrow for you, sorting through everything and listing what's there.'

Macey gave a satisfied sigh.

'Goodnight, then.'

Kerri, surprised that she accepted Leo's decision so easily, looked at him as he prepared to get back into the Volvo. He smiled at her, obviously thinking that perhaps Macey had found what she wanted now and would be content.

She wished she could believe that, too.

# Rescue

Rolling over in her sleep in the narrow camp bed, Kerri caught her injured thumb beneath her body and woke with a start into the grey light of dawn. For a painful moment she lay still until it gradually became bearable, leaving behind a dull ache she was beginning to become accustomed to. The nurse had said it would take time and to take it easy.

She yawned, wondering what the time was. Early yet, of course. Too early to get up? It was getting lighter by the minute now. She lay and listened to the silence and out there somewhere was the faint cry of a distant bird.

A hot drink would be good and a look outside, even a visit to her garden. The garden. She must remember that the garden wasn't hers in real life, only in her imagination. But that's where she wanted to be now, early as it was.

She pushed back the bedclothes and got out of bed. The bare floorboards felt cold as she padded across to the window to check that no low clouds smudged the view of the reservoir. Instead, the sky was pearly blue with a hint of hazy mauve on the horizon.

As she watched, two people emerged from the bird hide down near the water's edge. They stretched and then looked about them

170

for a moment or two before leaving. Kerri wondered if they had been there all night and hoped that they had seen something that made their vigil worthwhile.

She pulled on the clothes she had worn yesterday evening because they were close at hand, and went downstairs. While the kettle boiled she wiped away some smudges on the worktop and lined up the spare mugs. She felt as if she were putting things straight for the next occupants. But this wasn't a holiday cottage.

She carried her coffee outside and was in time to see the ornithologists' car drive slowly past the open gateway. They waved and she waved back with her bandaged hand, smiling as she set off across the yard.

It was strange that the gate had been left open at night, but stranger still for the outhouse door to be hanging on its hinges. There was something wrong here.

She stopped so suddenly that she hardly noticed that her coffee splashed out on to the cobbles. Then she walked towards the outhouse, afraid of what she would find, and saw the upturned boxes and the contents spilled out on to the floor. Macey and Damien wouldn't have left the place in this state. She stared in dismay, unable to move.

But she had to move. She had to report this, and the person to tell first was Damien.

He was beginning to stir as she knocked on

171

his bedroom door.

'What is it? What's the matter?'

'It's the outhouse. Someone's broken in!'

She went downstairs to wait and looked at her empty coffee mug in surprise. Then he was down, pulling on his jacket as he came in to the kitchen.

'Have you just discovered it?'

She nodded.

'Come and see.'

It was fully daylight now. They stood in the doorway and stared at the mess inside the outhouse.

'We left it tidy,' Damien said.

'Valuable things?'

He nodded.

'We put everything we took out back in the boxes.'

'Anything missing?'

'I can't tell yet.'

Kerri frowned.

'We'll have to tell Macey.'

Damien hesitated.

'I'd better check first.'

'No, don't touch anything.'

He looked at her helplessly and she knew what he was thinking. Macey had been so happy when they got back last evening. And now this! Telling her would be appalling.

'I'd better do it, then,' he said, but he didn't move.

'Somehow she'll blame me,' Kerri said.

172

The thought had obviously occurred to Damien, too, but it made no difference. They both knew it had to be done.

'It's early yet. She won't be up.'

Kerri felt in the pocket of her jeans.

'I'll phone the house if you like and tell her.'

'But there's no signal here.'

'I know a place to get a good one,' she said. 'At the top of the garden. I'll do it, because I discovered the damage. You put the kettle on, Damien.'

The garden seemed extra steep as Kerri climbed to the top, but she didn't pause until she got there. Several moments passed before Macey answered the phone and when she did she sounded bleary with sleep, annoyed that someone was phoning at this early hour. Kerri imagined her standing barefoot in the hall and shivering a little as she listened to what was being said.

Then the string of anger and accusations made Kerri reel. She held her phone away from her until Macey paused for breath and then turned it off and buried it deep in her pocket.

Breathing hard Kerri leaned against the shed wall, pressing into the hard surface behind her for strength. She wasn't surprised that Macey blamed her for what had happened, only that she had been unnecessarily vindictive. It was true, of course, that she couldn't prove her innocence but then why should she have to? Damien couldn't either, come to that, and neither could Macey herself.

That was a thought, and one that others might find interesting. Once it was known that Macey had hidden the silver jug and that it hadn't been stolen, it was a short step to thinking this break-in was her work, too.

Kerri gazed down over the overgrown garden to the house and beyond to the reservoir and the hills. She was unable to feel the peace of the awakening countryside because of Macey's bitter words.

On impulse she pulled out her phone again. Lucy would provide the instant sympathy and understanding she needed. When at last she reached her friend and spilled out the latest event that had shattered her confidence, Lucy's soft words were all that she could hope for.

'She needs to admit she took the jug herself. She hasn't done that, has she?' she said after she had commiserated with her at some length.

'That's the trouble. I don't think she will. But the evidence is all there.'

'Damien should make her admit it.'

'You don't know what she's like, Lucy.'

'Don't let her see that she's got to you.'

'I'll try not to.'

'And let me know how it goes. Promise? My phone will be switched on all day. Love you!'

She couldn't stay here at Alder Knowle

174

after this, Kerri thought with sudden resolve. Damien must make his own decision about what to do. She had had enough.

*       *       *

She heard voices from the kitchen and paused outside the door wondering whether to join her brother and Macey. But what would be the point? At any minute now Macey would come storming out to see the damage for herself. Then, presumably, there would be phone calls reporting what had happened. At some point Macey and Damien would have to see what was missing. And all the time the atmosphere would be filled with accusations against Kerri.

She left the yard and crossed the track, heading for the bird hide down by the water's edge. She needed time to think, to work out what she was going to do.

The hide was empty and she removed the branches that covered the entrance and went inside. She wondered for a moment if more lost articles would turn up here, and looked round to see. Nothing. This wasn't too surprising because the two boxfuls of things would take up space and would be heavy to carry over the stile and down the rough path.

She settled herself on the bench. Someone had left a large notebook open on the shelf in front of her and she saw that there were

175

columns for birds that had been spotted with space for the date and time and also for comments. Nothing had been seen during the night but there were notes about identifying various bird calls and a few tentative words about nightjars.

She turned back a page and saw that the meadow pipits had been entered. Someone had noted that at first they had been taken for rock pipits because the colour of their legs was slightly darker than usual. Here was proof in black and white that what she had told Leo was true about the morning that the silver jug was found.

But she didn't need proof, because he believed her. Damien did, too, and Annie and Lucy . . . all the people she cared about.

She gazed out at the peaceful scene in front of her, thinking of Leo and of how he had said he was keeping a look-out for Macey's wellbeing because of a promise he had made to his father. He was coming over here this Sunday morning anyway, but now he would have this latest development to deal with when he got here.

The sun was higher in the sky now and the slight rising breeze was sending glittering ripples across the calm water. She heard a squawk and a fluttering of wings somewhere near and strained forward for a better view.

She could see nothing but the waving strands of rushes. She watched for a few moments longer and then turned back to the notebook. But there it was again! This time she heard splashing and a high piping call, fainter this time. She could see something dark in the water. A bird? Of course it was but too far away to be identified by someone who knew little about water birds.

The pencil attached to the spine of the notebook by a piece of string was blunted after a lot of use. She wondered what she would note down if she was one of the ornithologists instead of the fugitive she felt herself to be.

This time the piping call was louder and she saw to her alarm that the bird, nearer now, seemed to be in trouble. Heart thudding, she sprang up and left the hide. The water on the edge was shallow, lapping gently on her feet. She might just be able to reach the poor thing if she was careful. Or at least see what was wrong with it and if it needed more help than she could give.

Quickly, she whipped off her shoes and socks and rolled up the legs of her jeans. The water was icy as Leo had said, but no matter. She took a step further and then another at the same time peering forward to get a better look at what was happening only a short distance from her. Another step and then she was floundering and trying in vain to regain her foothold on ground that fell steeply away. The resulting splash sent tidal waves of ripples further out into the reservoir and a streamlined bird rose in the air and winged its way off into the distance.

For a moment she felt the pull of her waterlogged clothes dragging at her and then, trying to keep her bandaged hand out of the water, she struck out in an awkward breast stroke.

The next moment she felt herself grabbed.

'What do you think you're doing?'

She gasped as Leo helped her to shallow water. On firm land she leaned against him, shaking. Her bandaged hand dripped water in spite of her attempts to keep it dry and her thumb hurt so much she hardly noticed that the rest of her was wet too and so was Leo.

She looked down at her bare feet, red with cold and shuddered.

'I tried to . . . I saw this bird. I thought I could save it.'

'Madness!' he said.

She knew that now. She breathed in the damp wool of his sweater, his skin and his hair.

'Come on, back to the cottage.' Releasing her, he picked up her shoes and socks. Then, before she could remonstrate, he picked her up, too, and stumbled with her to the stile and helped her over it.

A car drew up and she saw that it was the same one that Annie's brother had parked in the yard when he came to view the cottage the other day. Charles Brownley wasn't wearing a pink jacket now, but a khaki one with

178

waterproof trousers to match. He got out of the car and looked at them in annoyance.

His father emerged more slowly, throwing Kerri an anxious look. He had a pair of binoculars slung round his neck.

'We saw what happened' he said. 'We were following you along the track, Leo. We could see that someone was causing a commotion in the water.'

Leo straightened and looked at Kerri who stood drooping at his side.

'No real harm done apart from a soaking. I'll get her back to the cottage. And then get home and changed.'

'A black-throated diver was spotted to the south heading this way,' Derek Brownley said. 'That's why we're here.'

Charles looked at Kerri and frowned.

'And that was the bird you frightened away, rare in these parts.'

She was only too aware of that, and the shame was numbing. She had wanted to leave here earlier because of something she hadn't done. Now this had happened and she had ruined something that seemed of vital importance. She thought of that notebook in the hide waiting for something like this to be recorded. No doubt the new entry would have been starred in gold.

'Will it come back?' she asked through cold lips.

'Doubtful.' Charles Brownley frowned. 'It's

179

way off route. An opportunity lost.'

His father looked anxiously at Kerri as Leo made to pick her up again.

'No need for that, lad,' he said. 'The car's here. Charles can make himself useful. A drop of water won't hurt it. You get off home.'

Charles hesitated for a moment and then nodded. By the time he and Kerri had got in and he had reversed the vehicle into a suitable position to drive across the yard Leo had gone. The back door of the cottage stood open but there was no one there.

'You'll get a hot shower?' he asked.

She nodded.

'I will. And thanks.'

'We'll see you later.'

Was that a threat? She had been incredibly foolish. She thought of Leo's reaction to her involuntary swim.

The shower felt wonderful as the hot water cascaded over her in a steamy stream that was comforting. She stood under it for some time revelling in the warmth.

When she was dry again, dressed in her spare clothes and the sandals that had thankfully stayed dry, she dared to remove the soaked bandage from her hand. She was almost afraid to look at it but she soon saw that the swelling had gone down a little, but the place where they had drained her thumb looked red and raw. She found a clean tissue and wrapped it round as a temporary measure

180

and then set about towelling her hair. This wasn't easy with the use of only one hand and took longer that she had anticipated.

No-one was downstairs but there was a note in Damien's handwriting on the breakfast bar. She opened it.

*Kerri. Come over to the house when you're ready. Damien.*

That was clear enough, anyway, and she was hungry. They were in the kitchen, Damien eating toast and marmalade at the table and Macey pacing up and down.

'Where have you been?' she demanded.

'Charles Brownley and his father are down there in the bird hide,' Kerri said. 'I've just seen them.'

'Charles?' Macey stopped in mid-stride. 'Does that mean you thought you'd find more missing things there?'

Kerri sat down at the table and reached for a slice of bread.

'You know what's missing, then?'

'We checked one box so far,' Damien said. 'The police needed to know. We'll have to do the other before they get here.'

'So it's true?' she said. 'There was a real break-in. Does that mean I'm in the clear?'

Damien smiled at her.

'You always have been, as far as I'm concerned.'

Macey scowled at him.

'All right. I admit it. I put the jug in the bird

hide. It was mine and the hide is on my land.'

'Why?' Damien looked up.

'Yes, why, Macey?'

Macey shrugged.

'Why does anyone do anything? Or not do anything? Like not selling this house to someone who wants it . . .'

'You mean the cottage?' Kerri asked.

Macey looked at her with loathing.

'What's it to you?'

Kerri put down her knife, no longer hungry.

'I need some sort of bandage. Have you got anything suitable? This tissue's no good. It keeps slipping off and I'm afraid the wound will get infected.'

Damien looked concerned.

'What happened to the other?'

'It got wet.'

'I've nothing here that will do any good,' Macey said. Kerri didn't wait for more. As she left she was aware of Damien getting to his feet but didn't linger to find out where he was going. She felt lonelier at this moment than she had done for a long time. She hardly knew what to do except go to the place where she always felt content.

In the sunshine the garden looked beautiful because there were strands of silver cobwebs on the brambles. She breathed in the smell of autumn and as she climbed she pulled the tissues on her thumb more tightly round it and held them in place with her fingers. She needed only one hand here in this quiet place.

Instead of getting out a garden chair she perched on the ridge at the bottom of the wall and looked down over the house and the yard. In the distance the reservoir glittered but she didn't, at the moment, wish to be reminded of something that made her hot with embarrassment.

A robin twittered nearby and regarded her speculatively. This, at least, was a bird she recognised. One day she might learn more about bird life and discover what the fascination was in sitting for hours in a cramped space in the hope of seeing something rare and interesting. But somehow she didn't think so.

She heard a car down below but she wasn't going to move. It approached slowly and then drove past the gateway and out of sight. Then, a few moments later, it returned and parked.

Two people got out and walked into the yard. Annie and Lucy! For a stunned moment Kerri could only stare in astonishment.


## Lucy Arrives

Kerri didn't know where Macey and Damien were, and was relieved that neither appeared as she ran through the garden to the yard.

183

'Lucy?'

They flew into each other's arms.

'Oh, Lucy, I'm so glad to see you.'

'Me, too.' Lucy's smile, as they broke apart, seemed to light up her surroundings. Then it faded again as she looked around her, clearly expecting to catch a glimpse of someone she would rather not see.

'But what are you doing here?' Kerri asked.

'Not a very friendly welcome for your best friend,' Annie commentated.

'I heard the anguish in your voice, Kerri. I had to come.'

'So quickly!' Kerri marvelled.

Lucy smiled.

'I'm staying with my aunt in Nottingham so it was quite straightforward most of the way.'

'Brilliant.'

'I stopped back there in a place called Alderfield and asked for directions for the last part. Annie was there and said she'd show me.'

Kerri, aware that the other two might appear at any moment, looked anxiously at Lucy's car parked on the other side of the track. Before she could suggest moving it to a less conspicuous place she heard voices, Damien's disbelieving and Macey's distinctly annoyed. It was too late to escape.

'Who are you?' Macey demanded as she advanced towards them.

'This is our friend, Lucy,' Kerri said. 'Lucy, this is Macey Treghennel, who owns all this.'

184

'The long-lost relative?'

Macey frowned.

'Why are you here?'

'Kerri told me there was a problem.'

'Problem?' Macey glanced at Damien as he leaned against the wall, his face pale. He was staring at Lucy as if he couldn't see enough of her.

'Her injury, for a start,' Lucy said. 'That's why I came. She needs someone on her side.'

'Me for one,' Annie said, determined not to be forgotten.

'I won't have that girl on my property, or Annie either.' Macey's words seemed to hang on the deep silence that followed.

'I have no intention of staying.' Lucy spoke with dignity.

'And neither will I. I can get packed in minutes, Lucy.'

Kerri took a deep breath to gain control of her voice. Her integrity was at stake here. She had done her best to protect Damien from making a huge mistake, but what right had she to assume she knew best for her brother?

Macey's face lit up.

'So, Damien. It looks as if we shall be on our own at last.'

He looked at her steadily for a long moment in which Kerri hardly dare breathe.

'I don't think so,' he said at last, his voice deadly quiet. Macey looked from one to the other.

'What do you mean?'

'Lucy and I have a lot to talk about.'

'You promised to look after my interests!'

'I'm glad to have been of help.'

'Help? I want more than help!' Macey cried.

'And that's what you'll be getting,' a voice said from behind them.

Macey spun round.

'You?'

'Indeed me,' Charles Brownley said pleasantly. 'Enough of this shilly-shallying. The sale of the house goes through as well as the cottage, as we agreed before this play-acting. Right?'

'The break-in last night was genuine,' she said in a sulky tone of voice.

He raised his eyebrows.

'I'll believe you.'

'But nothing was taken,' Damien broke in. 'We've just checked.'

Kerri could see that Annie was holding her breath. But her brother hadn't finished.

'We have purchasers for both properties, willing to pay the full asking price. Take it, and you're free of financial worries. Live a little. Go on a cruise. And when you return we'll get together and see what happens.'

Macey nodded too overcome to speak.

Charles smiled and then looked at Annie as if surprised to see her there.

'Dad's in the hide if you want to join him.'

'He'll give me a lift back.' Annie winked at

Kerri.

'He'd better collect Mum and they can have a look at the cottage. That's in order, isn't it, Macey?'

'If you say so, Charles,' she said meekly.

Damien was still looking at Lucy.

'You came all this way to rescue Kerri?'

'Two and a half hours from Auntie Joan's place,' Lucy said, looking pleased with herself.

'You're a marvel,' Damien told her.

'And so are you. I know that now. I have done for days. I didn't know what I should do. I'm so, so sorry. And then Kerri phoned.'

Damien's smile was wide.

'You really mean it?'

They gazed at each other and Lucy looked radiant.

Happy for them, Kerri turned away and looked at Annie.

'I owe your dad an apology,' she said.

'Not to worry,' Annie said. 'He and Mum will have too much to think about with the move. And I shall insist they offer you accommodation if you need to stay in the area, Kerri. Now, your thumb . . .'

Kerri looked down at it and saw that the tissue was working loose.

'I'd forgotten that.'

'I saw Leo just now. He said something about being on hospital duty this morning. So I will see you around.' And Annie was gone.

When Leo came, he looked so distinguished

in his navy sweatshirt and jeans that Kerri's heart lurched. He leaped out of his car and came towards her, smiling.

She got up from her seat on the low wall where she had been waiting since the others left.

'Leo?'

'I came as soon as I could. All alone?' He glanced behind her at the silent house, the curtains pulled halfway across all the windows.'

'Damien and Lucy didn't want to leave me here,' she said. 'But I insisted and they seemed to understand. They went off half an hour ago, to stay with Lucy's aunt. Then to Cornwall, as it's Lucy's half term.'

'It seems I've missed all the action. Annie was jubilant at the way things have turned out. She's a great girl.'

'Soon to be homeless.'

'I think Max has some ideas about that. And Macey and Charles?'

'I didn't realise Charles was so masterful.'

'Macey will appreciate that.'

'She does. She's all dewy-eyed and friendly. She's given me some things for Damien—some alabaster bookends he admired, a horribly ugly Toby jug he fancied, and a set of old-fashioned silver cutlery that belonged to our great great grandfather. They're packed up with my stuff in the cottage.'

His smile faded.

'You're leaving?'

'Only to the Brownleys' place, temporarily. Annie's arranging it. My reservoir swim didn't do me any harm after all.'

She laughed rather shakily, still unable to believe Derek Brownley's generous reaction.

'Certainly not with me. You're a great girl, too, Kerri.'

She flushed with pleasure.

He took her injured hand in his.

'Can I see?'

'It's not nice.'

Gently he pulled back the tissues and she flinched a little as her wound was exposed.

'It's healing,' he said as he covered it again.

She could almost feel it happening because Leo had said so and she trusted him implicitly.

'So it's Outpatients first. And then I'm going to take you off somewhere amazing, to ask you something . . .'

'Don't tell me—those wonderful rock formations?'

'Those first, yes, and then we'll come back to somewhere even more amazing.' His eyes shone. 'Guess where? Here, to this place behind us.'

She turned to look at the house that stood back from the road with the expanse of lawn in front of it and she now knew, the walled garden behind so full of promise.

'I was going to wait to ask you something important but now I find I can't.' His voice faltered.

She moved towards him and was immediately in his arms. He bent to kiss her and it was the most wonderful moment of her life. She felt drowned in happiness and the next moment her heart was soaring.

When at last he released her he was smiling.

'I can't imagine life without you. I love you. Together we can make such a success of our lives in this place—our own horticultural business, special residential courses . . .'

'I feel we could make a success of anything, you and I,' she murmured. 'Given time.'

'But not ornithology! And just to remind us, I've saved this.' He pulled something from his pocket.

She laughed as she saw the small white jug, decorated with a painting of a duck.

# Chivers Large Print Direct

If you have enjoyed this Large Print book and would like to build up your own collection of Large Print books and have them delivered direct to your door, please contact **Chivers Large Print Direct**.

**Chivers Large Print Direct** offers you a full service:

☆ **Created to support your local library**

☆ **Delivery direct to your door**

☆ **Easy-to-read type and attractively bound**

☆ **The very best authors**

☆ **Special low prices**

For further details either call Customer Services on 01225 443400 or write to us at

**Chivers Large Print Direct**
**FREEPOST (BA 1686/1)**
**Bath**
**BA1 3QZ**